My Guide Inside

Knowing Myself and Understanding My World
(Book III)
Advanced, Secondary Learner Book

Christa Campsall
with
Kathy Marshall Emerson

3 Principles Ed Talks
myguideinside.com

CCB Publishing
British Columbia, Canada

My Guide Inside (Book III) Advanced, Secondary Learner Book

Copyright © 2016, 2017, 2020, 2024 by Christa Campsall - http://www.myguideinside.com
My Guide Inside® is a registered trademark of Christa Campsall (3 Principles Ed Talks)
ISBN-13   978-1-77143-593-2
Second Edition

Library and Archives Canada Cataloguing in Publication
Title: My guide inside (book III) advanced, secondary learner book / by Christa Campsall with Kathy Marshall Emerson.
Names: Campsall, Christa, author.
Issued in print and electronic formats.
ISBN 9781771435932 (softcover) | ISBN 9781771435949 (PDF)
Additional cataloguing data available from Library and Archives Canada

Authored with: Kathy Marshall Emerson
Editing: Jane Tucker
Conceptual Development: Barbara Aust, Kathy Marshall Emerson
Production: Tom Tucker
Contributions: Jane Tucker, Kathy Marshall Emerson, Bob Campsall, Mavis Karn, Paul Lock, Braden Hughs
Graphic Design: Josephine Aucoin
Webmaster: Michael Campsall
Images: Shutterstock.com

E-books, MGI Online, Video on Demand Classes, Video Clips, and Digital Media Tools:
See www.**myguideinside.com** for information on these resources.

The author has taken extreme care to ensure that all information in this book is accurate and current at the time of publication. Neither the author nor the publisher can be held responsible for any errors or omissions. Likewise, no liability is assumed for any damage caused by the use of the information from this publication.

All rights reserved. No part of this work may be reproduced in any form – graphically, electronically or mechanically – or processed, duplicated or distributed using electronic systems without the written permission of the author, except for reviewers who may quote brief passages. Any request for photocopying, recording, taping or storage in information systems for any part of this work should be made in writing to the author at: **myguideinside.com**

Why an Owl? Over the years as a classroom teacher, Christa was given various owl gifts. She loves them as symbols of the wisdom we all share. Starting in ancient times and throughout history, various cultures have seen the owl as linked with wisdom and guidance. The owl's big, round eyes symbolize seeing knowledge. Although it is sometimes linked to other ideas, it is because of this connection to wisdom, guidance, and seeing knowledge that the owl was chosen as the graphic symbol for *My Guide Inside (MGI)*. Christa hopes this interpretation is also meaningful to you. One of Christa's former students, Jo Aucoin, now a graphic artist, was commissioned to create the *My Guide Inside* owl and clouds. The orange clouds graphic was chosen to symbolize daybreak as you transition into adulthood.

Publisher: CCB Publishing
              British Columbia, Canada
              www.ccbpublishing.com

My Guide Inside® (Learner Book III)

Table of Contents

Is *My Guide Inside* worth your time?...iv
Foreword...v

Learning the Foundation
Chapter 1 Discovering *My Guide Inside*..1
Chapter 2 The Lure of Being Secure..9

Learning from Life
Chapter 3 Flawsome and Fun: Our True Identity...19
Chapter 4 Living in the Present: Leaving the Past in the Dust....................27
Chapter 5 Understanding the Lost Thinker..41
Chapter 6 Making Room for Happiness...50
Chapter 7 Facing the Future in a State of Well-being.................................61

Moving Forward
Chapter 8 Defining Your Individual Path..68

Teens Have the Last Word!..72
Appendices..73
Appendix A: Learner *MGI* III Pre-Assessment..74
Appendix B: Learner *MGI* III Post-Assessment..75
Appendix C: Lesson Reminders from *My Guide Inside*® (Book II)...............76
Appendix: D Lesson Reminders from *My Guide Inside*® (Book III)............77
Appendix E: Guidance for Peer Counselors and Peer Mentors....................80
Appendix F: Vital Vocabulary A-Z..81
Appendix G: Works Cited..85
Acknowledgments...88
About the Authors...89
Overview of *My Guide Inside* Comprehensive Curriculum..........................89

DOCUMENT YOUR REAL CHANGE!

Before beginning, please complete the Learner Pre-Assessment. At the conclusion of this class, check your growth by completing Learner Post-Assessment.

Enjoy your learning journey!

My Guide Inside® (Learner Book III)

Is My Guide Inside worth your time?

You may want to consider what other teens have reported:

⚜ "I was surprised that the solutions to the situations we talked about actually worked!"

⚜ "I got suspended before I found out some of this … I actually punched a kid … But then I found out it was a separate reality thing and it could've been stopped."

⚜ "This class has helped me a lot. I have enjoyed it. I hope we can do it next year. This class will help me all the way through my life. Thank you."

⚜ "Most of my thoughts are positive now, even when I don't get my way because I understand how the other person looks at it, in a different perspective. My relationship with my parents is better. I'm not trying to prove anything anymore."

⚜ "To forgive is the best feeling of all. Don't let the negative thoughts control your life."

⚜ "I used quiet mind because I didn't do any of my homework and I had a ton to do the next day. So I did it all in school. Just kind of calmed myself down at the end of the day and did a bunch. Got it all done. I was proud of myself."

⚜ "The most valuable aspect would have to be learning about Thought and state of mind because I now know that thoughts are what you make them. It also has helped me to stop analyzing negative thoughts and know how to prevent them by being positive. It works. Thanks!"

⚜ "I learned about Three Principles in school about 15 years ago and this knowledge is still the foundation of my life today!" (From a former teen, now an adult)

Real Teens, Real Change

See what kids and teens think by watching two videos at myguideinside.com. *My Guide Inside* Overview (5min) and *My Guide Inside* Secondary Students Outcomes (5min).

Teens like you made these comments and many other important contributions to this book. Special gratitude goes to the those who kindly shared their authentic *Teen Reflections* in each chapter. Others were in focus groups, gave feedback and made brilliant suggestions. **My Guide Inside** has stories written for you based on accounts of real changes in young people who learned the principles. These stories were written by Jane Tucker and Christa Campsall, who both saw similar positive changes while working with young people at various times and at opposite sides of the North American continent.

My Guide Inside® (Learner Book III)

Foreword

Students report *My Guide Inside* preparation for life after high school.

We asked how *MGI* impacted student lives three years later from 2018 to 2021:

"Something that carried over has definitely been continuous change: living in different places, going to different schools, learning different things. Change is the most consistent thing. Practicing and remembering that you have to check in with yourself are key."

"*MGI* principles are universal and definitely ingrained in how I live my life. The fundamental spirit of what we were learning is both awareness of self and compassion for others."

"Whenever I am really in a bad mood I just try to take a step back and understand what is going on. I learned a lot from that *MGI* course three years ago."

"At work during the pandemic I really saw people struggling. I would reach out and just make sure that they were okay. I am glad I have this background so I can help other people."

"After high school I studied in an international program. What we learned from *MGI* really enabled me to know the best way to approach people who have never had the opportunity to talk about themselves."

"*MGI* has taught me many valuable lessons I use frequently in my life and nursing practice."

"*MGI* led me to be self-aware and progress in breaking my own implicit biases."

Three years after the *MGI* class students were confident in knowing how to naturally keep themselves in a healthy calm state of mind, to gain employment, make and even change career or university decisions. Furthermore, they did so during the very difficult time of the global pandemic and widespread isolation. Perhaps, most importantly, they report being in service to others: listening, caring, contacting and supporting fellow students, family members, customers, and others.

Objectives of My Guide Inside

This **MGI** curriculum points the way to wholeness, happiness, creativity and well-being in all parts of your life.

Therefore, **MGI** has these two academic goals: (1) to enhance your Personal Well-being with an understanding of these principles, and (2) to develop your competencies in Communication, Thinking, and Personal and Social Responsibility. **MGI** accomplishes both goals by using stories, discussion and various written and creative activities, as the learning increases your competency in English Language Arts, including Digital Media.

Discovering your guide inside, key to learning, enhances your ability to make decisions, navigate your life and build healthy relationships. Accessing natural wisdom will affect your well-being, spiritual wellness, personal and social responsibility, and positive personal and cultural identity. We start by uploading happiness.

Chapter 1
Discovering My Guide Inside

*Discovering **My Guide Inside**, inner wisdom, leads to happiness and understanding. Everyone has mental health inside, also defined as a state of well-being. Learning three principles shows how we create our own personal experience of life from the inside-out. Understanding an equation points us to mental well-being and helps us find our bearings:*

*"**Mind + Consciousness + Thought = Reality**"* (Enl.G.R. 42)

*Exploring the logic of separate realities helps us communicate clearly with others. There's comic relief in seeing separate realities in action! Gaining knowledge of our **Guide Inside** enables us to live a life filled with happiness and well-being. As one teen remarked, "The Three Principles are like your decoder ring!"*

This chapter introduces the Three Principles. These principles are the foundation of MGI. This is the opportunity for you to discover your own Guide Inside that points each of us to natural insights and happiness.

Uploading Happiness

Think of a time you felt happy and secure. Do you feel happy now? Even though you may temporarily feel unhappy at times, you can get your smile back!

A Little History

Did you know psychologists all over the world have been trying hard to understand human psychology for a very long time? Sydney Banks was not a psychologist but an ordinary man who simply saw principles operating in himself and wanted to share his findings with all people, especially psychologists. He explained that William James, one of the fathers of modern psychology, … "had an insight that somewhere inside of everybody lay mental health, but he couldn't prove it. … he did say that hopefully someday, somewhere, somebody would discover principles that would change psychology from a personal philosophy into a working science. And I honestly believe that we have found those principles; the principles of Mind, Consciousness and Thought." (Att. 4:52)

Equation for Happiness

Gaining an understanding of these three principles, three truths, leads to happiness! These principles are true for every person on earth. You might think of this as the ***Three Principles Equation***:

"Mind + Consciousness + Thought = Reality" (Enl.G.R. 42)

Author Sydney Banks realized we all operate from the inside-out. He cared deeply about young people and knew that if we could help you understand this, the world would be a far, far better place. He said, "The way I see it … we were given three special gifts to assist us through life. They are Universal Mind, which is the source of all intelligence, Universal Consciousness, which allows us to be aware of our existence, and Universal Thought, which guides us through the world we live in as free-thinking agents." (Enl. 38)

Inside of every person, you and me included, Mind, Consciousness and Thought work together to create the reality we each experience. We, as thinkers, can change our reality from happiness to unhappiness or from unhappiness to happiness. What we do with a thought is the variable that makes a difference.

Power of Choice

Just because a thought pops into your head doesn't mean you have to go along with it. You are not a robot! A thought needs your attention to stay alive. We have free will to choose, in the moment, which thoughts to ignore, and which thoughts to entertain. Because we instantly feel what we think, we are able to naturally and effortlessly make a good choice when we listen for a feeling—listen to our guide inside.

My Guide Inside® (Learner Book III)

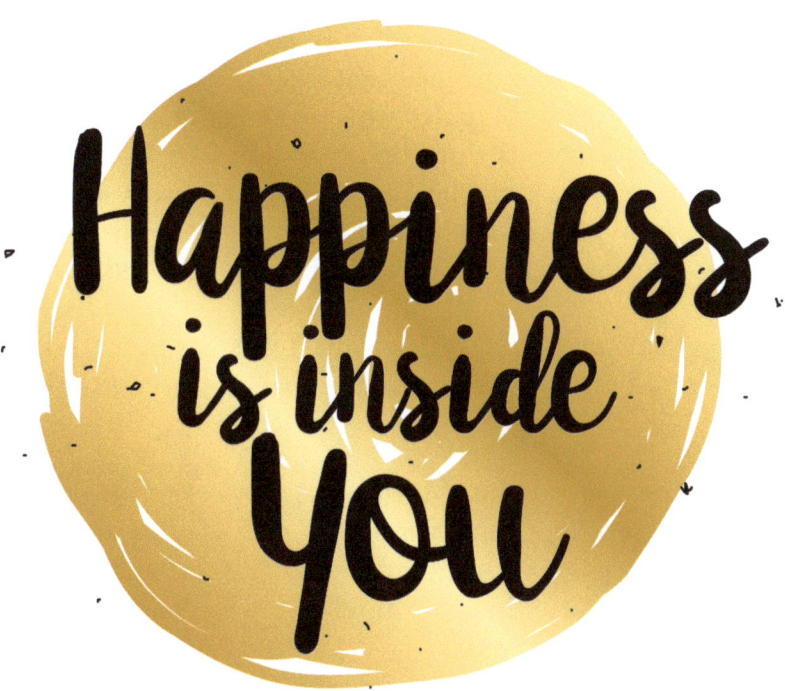

"The happiness you're looking for is inside you. It really is. That's where mental health lies." (One 1:27) Use your guide inside to upload happiness and navigate your world with "healthy thoughts from moment-to-moment." (Mis. 4) This creates mental health; defined as a state of well-being.

Your Decoder Ring

One teen called these Three Principles your *Decoder Ring*. He saw that he (like everyone) has the power to unlock the code to his experiences—Thought working with Mind and Consciousness to create his reality. He said, "Once you know about the Three Principles, you see the real truth of it everywhere, which helps you to navigate your world." Like that young man, you can crack the code and see *your reality* is created by *your thinking* in the moment. Once you know *Thought* is the link, you can never un-know it. This "knowledge will come via a feeling." (Gre.S. 15:55) It's a game changer.

➢ **Think, pair, share**
- Talk about the "Three Principles Equation" or "Your Decoder Ring."

Realizing Wisdom

What is a good name for inner wisdom? Wisdom is "an inner intelligence which everyone is born with." (Att. Part 2 1:00) It is the inner intelligence we are discovering together! We are not referring to the brain, a biological computer, which is sometimes called the *personal mind*. Instead we refer to the source of innate intelligence within all of us, known as the *principle of Mind*. No matter how smart we are or where we are on our journey of life, there is no end to learning from this universal principle of Mind. Fascinating! It is a definite asset to know that Mind/Wisdom/Inner Intelligence, is always available to us. (24/7/365).

How do you describe wisdom beyond your personal thinking? In this book, my *Guide Inside* refers to natural wisdom. There are various phrases that have been used by others:

Common sense	Inner intelligence	Knowing
Guide Inside	Inner wisdom	Little voice inside
Innate health	Insight	Mind
Innate wisdom	Intuitive mind	Natural wisdom

Is there a term you would like to add? Use the phrase you like; take ownership of your learning. What are the top three choices of the group?

My Guide Inside is about helping you know yourself and understand your world.

➢ **Let's talk about the big picture.**
- Are these facts or fallacies about inner intelligence or wisdom? Share what new ideas occur to you.

~Fact: "Start feeling good about yourself [and] this wisdom will come out." (Att. 12:05)
~Fallacies: "Wisdom comes from age and … wisdom comes from the outside in." (Att. 11:40)

Teen Reflections: How do these resonate with you?

"I have learned to use my common sense more and my own judgment to make it easier on myself. Overall, knowing about my natural inner wisdom has given me more confidence in myself, life and in the future."

"In my life I used to find it difficult to let go of my vision of how things should go. During this time, I've learned that if we let go of our right versus wrong attitude and accept each other's ideas as valid then we are able to relate on a clear level."

My Guide Inside® (Learner Book III)

The Personal Movie: Appreciating Separate Realities

What *we do* with a thought is the variable that makes a difference. It results in us each having independent thoughts, therefore we each "see a separate reality." (Mis. 6) Even while sharing an experience with others, each person creates their own movie.

- ➢ **Think, pair, share: Choose to talk about the "personal movies" or "separate realities" individuals experience. Share answers to these questions:**
    ~What might each person be thinking as they look at the sunset and water?
    ~What are your own thoughts when you look at the same scene?
    ~What feeling might wash over you?
    ~How can knowledge about separate realities be of benefit as you navigate your world?

MGI Chapter Resource Center

Use the resources, activities and projects provided to enhance your learning.
- **Activities**: These are for credit, grades and creativity. Use the criteria for success!
- **Just for Fun**: Enjoy a good feeling.
- **Vital Vocabulary**: Enhance communication.
- **Experiment**: Try this during the week.
- **Appendix D**: "Reminders" deepen understanding.
- **Resources Tab**: myguideinside.com includes Video On Demand to bring this chapter to life, Video Clips that enhance, and Digital Media Options for each activity. Password: mgi

Activities

❖ **Reflect and Write a Journal Entry**
- Create an *MGI* journal. Write a reflection or respond to one of these ideas; include Vital Vocabulary words.

  "I am happy and content because I think I am." (Alain Le Sage)

  "The happiness you're looking for is inside you. It really is. That's where mental health lies." (One 1:27)

  Success Criteria: use "I," share thoughts, feelings; show insight, connections.

❖ **Respond to a Video Clip**
- Respond in your journal.
  See Resources tab.
  Success Criteria: use "I," express your ideas clearly; show insight, connections.

❖ **Think of a Time**
- Think of a time when you experienced happiness doing something you enjoyed. Think about what you were doing, where you were, who you were with and how you were feeling. Fortunately, happiness is not just for when you're doing something special. Add a conclusion about your potential for happiness. Write about how your thinking related to your feeling of happiness. Remember, the way you choose to use *Thought* is the key variable leading to your own happiness.

  Success Criteria: focused central idea, meaningful text shows depth of thought, logical sequence, clear language and correct conventions, engaging voice is evident.

❖ **Create a Work of Art**
- Create a picture to enhance your writing for *Think of a Time*.
  Success Criteria: be original and creative, show skillful use of materials, be expressive and detailed, and use space effectively.

❖ **Create a Banner**
- Use a key phrase or related slogan to create a banner to display or share online. <u>Or</u> use one of these examples: Discover **My Guide Inside**, **MGI**: Key to Happiness; It's a Thought-Created World.

Success Criteria: be clear and expressive, accurate and neat, use the space effectively and make it colorful.

Just for Fun

✓ **Enjoy a Video Clip** …
Happy Song by Pharrell Williams. (Length 4:06)

✓ **Comic Relief** … Comedy in action happens because of separate realities. Sitcoms are based on separate realities. Share examples of separate realities creating comedy in your life or in shows you have seen. Laughter is good medicine!

✓ **Enjoy a Sunset Viewing** … Appreciate the beauty of nature, by yourself, with another or a number of others. Make time to reflect. You'll be amazed at what insights might occur to you!

Vital Vocabulary

Some of these words are relatively simple.
Understanding them in a deeper way will enhance your communication.

Compassion—feeling of empathy
Common sense—knowing to make good choices, insight, my guide inside, wisdom
Consciousness—awareness, uppercase "C" denotes the principle
Fallacy—failure in reasoning
Free will—ability to choose which thought to act on
Guide—wise and knowing adviser, helps to navigate life
Happiness—well-being and contentment, a sense that life has meaning
Innate—intuitive and natural
Insight—a helpful new idea, common sense, my guide inside, wisdom
Intuitive—innate and natural
Invigorate—give energy to
Logical—makes common sense
Mental health—state of well-being
Metaphor—symbol of something else
Mind—source of intelligence, uppercase "M" denotes the principle
My guide inside—common sense, insight, wisdom
Personal—belonging to a particular person
Principle—truth, foundation for a chain of reasoning
Reality—how life looks to the thinker
Reasoning—thinking about something in a logical way
State—condition or way of being that exists at a particular time
Thought—creative tool, capacity to think, uppercase "T" denotes the principle

Understand—to know
Universal—belonging to all people
Understanding—using compassion and kindness as guides; awareness
Variable—something that may vary or change that influences an outcome
Well-being—tate of being comfortable, healthy and happy; overall satisfaction with life
Wisdom—knowing what is true or right, common sense, insight, my guide inside

Experiment

Throughout the week, notice you can and do have good feelings. Are you happy and content at any time when you're not doing something special?

Chapter 2
The Lure of Being Secure

Everyone wants to feel secure. Insecure feelings can show up in many ways; they wear many different masks. If your head is full of negative thoughts, you will feel insecure. In that state of mind, you experience low moods and in some limited cases even depression. But you are in charge; there is a solution! You have free will to choose which thoughts to pay attention to or "bring to life."

If you are open to it, you can actually see what is going on inside of you. You will learn you are drawn to good feelings and you will actually gravitate to a secure state. When your negative thoughts fall away—when you just let them pass—you will return to a natural feeling of security and enjoy life more. The bonus is you will become grateful and that actually increases your sense of security. One teen explains, "Disguises of insecurity are the masks we put on when we are feeling uneasy … Learning Three Principles has helped me to be more secure about myself and my relationships."

This chapter completes the MGI introduction to the basic foundation of the principles. You will explore the relationship of Thought, feeling and a secure state of mind, and use intelligence and innate wisdom in communicating your own new viewpoints in relationships with others.

Lee's Story
What clues about Lee's Story are revealed in the chapter title?

Lee knew all about moving. When he was little he thought everybody moved a lot, but as he got older he realized most kids didn't change schools every year or two. The first few times, his dad was transferred. Then he was offered a better job, and they moved again. Not long after, that company closed and everyone was laid off. The moving just did not stop.

Lee understood they had to go where the work was and knew he had a lot to be grateful for. His dad always managed to find something that kept their little family (just the two of them) comfortable enough. Lee had friends who weren't so lucky. He didn't really mind changing schools, especially at the beginning of the school year. His dad did his best to make changes then.

From a young age, Lee found different localities interesting; his natural friendliness and curiosity about others kept him from being an "outsider" at any school for very long. He was adaptable and had a knack for picking up regional accents, quickly sounding like a "local." He found it easy to fit in.

When Lee was 14, after completing his second year at the same school, his dad said he wanted to talk with him about something important. Lee had a feeling—it was like "déjà vu." He was pretty sure another change was in the works. His dad assured him this would be a great move with a solid promotion, and even included housing. It meant college might even be a real possibility for Lee one day. The 300-mile (480 km) move, at the end of the month, would allow plenty of time to settle in before school started again.

Lee felt like a lead weight had landed on him. He felt utterly unprepared and unwilling to move again. Anxious thoughts flooded Lee's mind as he imagined having to meet a whole school full of new people. He had never felt like this; he was uncharacteristically worried about "fitting in." At the same time, he realized this really was a great opportunity for them, and knew they would have to go.

The month rushed by with packing and spending as much time as possible hanging out with his friends for the last time. In spite of his history of easily making friends wherever he went, Lee feared this time he was different, and that he wouldn't know how to act in another, unfamiliar environment.

As Lee and his father settled into their new home, worries kept Lee inside the apartment feeling low and too shy to approach teens at the park across the street. He spent hours online, checking out what everyone from his last school was posting, messaging his old friends, and thinking about the good times he was missing out on.

∞

Lee was preoccupied with thoughts of self-doubt and by the time school started, he actually felt tongue-tied. The more anxious he became, the more he had seemingly endless reasons for being insecure.

Lee was in despair, spiraling into depression. He didn't know where his "personality" had gone. He thought he'd had all the fun he was ever going to have in life, and figured he was doomed to being sad and lonely. He had never been so isolated. He felt caught in a vicious cycle.

Lee's social life that school year was miserable. His dad tried to help him by sharing something he was learning at work-- a new way of looking at things.

His company was learning to see how Mind, Consciousness and Thought work together to create our personal reality; this perspective was helping employees and management understand each other better. "I don't comprehend it fully," he told his son. "I never realized this before but when we are in touch with our own common sense and wisdom, we can *feel* when our thinking is taking us off track. This wisdom helps us see these thoughts for what they are—just illusions that separate us. We can feel less gripped by our thinking and use our free will to choose to stop feeding unproductive thoughts."

These words didn't seem to have an effect on Lee at the time, although he appreciated his dad caring enough to want to help him. Lee clung to the thought that he had somehow become a shy, insecure person. It was now his belief.

When school let out for the summer, Lee landed a job minding three little boys while their parents were at work. These kids were so lively that Lee came home every day exhausted! He would sink into a chair and just sit there enjoying how quiet it was in contrast to racing after the boys all day.

While catching his breath Lee realized how satisfied he felt. He didn't desire a thing! When anxiety began nagging him he let these thoughts pass by. He just enjoyed the feeling of satisfaction at the end of each day.

It began to dawn on Lee that he had set himself up to be lonely and isolated by the way he'd acted and felt so sorry for himself during the last school year. He remembered his dad's words: "We can use our free will and choose to stop feeding thoughts that aren't productive and keep us feeling low." Could it be he'd been innocently "feeding" thoughts like "I'm shy, I'm different, I can't fit in"? Had he actually created the very thing he'd been so afraid of? Hmmmm ...

Lee had a good summer, tiring as it was. Right before school started he and his dad went away for several days, hiking on a wilderness trail and camping by a waterfall that fed into a perfect pool for swimming. It had been years since they had done anything like this. Lee saw his dad with new eyes—not just as his parent, but as a friend. He couldn't remember a better vacation.

When classes resumed, the insecure thoughts that seemed so real the previous year fell away. To his surprise, he got to know more people during the first month of this year than he had the entire year before.

As the semester continued, Lee became busier and busier. He got involved in sports and clubs and spent a lot of time with the many new friends he'd made. He was amazed how witty he had become. He could always get people laughing! Life was full.

One weekend afternoon, after a long driving lesson, Lee flopped down on the living room chair to enjoy his cold drink. He was glad to have a break. He ignored thoughts of texting someone or making plans and just basked in the feeling of taking it easy.

Remembering hobbies he'd developed, Lee realized he hadn't spent any time on his own in ages. He wondered if maybe he had taken the idea of being popular and outgoing too far.

Another uncomfortable realization suddenly hit him. Once he'd seen how he could "draw a crowd" with his off-the-wall sense of humor, he'd gotten into a habit of making subtle (or sometimes not so subtle) jokes at others' expense. Deep down, he knew this was unkind and hurtful, but had ignored that inner voice of conscience. He had to keep it up for fear he might be ignored and lonely again.

Lee felt embarrassed when he realized what he'd been doing. He remembered his dad saying inner wisdom lets us know when our thinking is taking us off track--basically we just don't feel right. That inner voice (whatever name it goes by) was now coming through loud and clear, and Lee knew he could change.

Lee started to reflect on something else he hadn't wanted to acknowledge; his grades were really suffering this year. For months, he'd been ignoring a "gut feeling" that he shouldn't be going out when there was an assignment to do. However, he had thought of this as "the price you have to pay" for being popular. Lee realized he'd gotten so caught up that he'd gotten things all out of perspective.

It was clear to Lee that both his "Shy Guy" and "Mr. Popular" images were just personae, fueled by mistaken thinking. They weren't who he really was. His own thinking had tricked him twice.

The first time, he'd thought leaving his old school meant he wouldn't have any friends, and that became his insecure reality. After the summer, when he discovered he didn't have to keep feeding "unproductive" thoughts, they fell away and he had more confidence.

But now he was seeing just how subtle the game of life could be; his thoughts had tricked him again. Somehow he had started to believe that if he didn't maintain his image of being popular, no matter what the cost, his world would fall apart. It was just insecure thinking in a different disguise.

∞

Like fresh air flowing into a stuffy room, insight about who he was and what he really wanted became clear to him. He didn't want to keep trying to impress everybody, going full speed with one thing after another. He found the determination and courage to be true to himself and do what felt right at the time—whether that was hanging out with a few good friends, or whatever.

As a beginning driver, Lee couldn't help thinking how, in some ways, life was like operating a car. Just as texting can distract us and cause driving accidents, mistaken thoughts can distract us from what's really going on. Fortunately, we're all equipped with an internal GPS—a guide inside that leads us in the right direction when we let go of insecure thinking.

Lee was grateful to see he was the one steering his car of life. His inner wisdom was always available to guide him back on track. Lee settled back in the chair, feeling better than he had in a long time.

➤ **Let's talk about the big picture.**
- This story about Lee may or may not relate to your experience, but the logic of free will and choice is always the same. How is the logic in this story like something you know?
- Talk about Lee's insight and how it relates to this: "No one can give away wisdom. A teacher can only lead you to it via words, hoping you will have the courage to look within yourself." (Mis. 128)

Masks of Insecurity

Take a look at the list below and see if you can relate to any of these insecurity personae or "masks." Have the courage to have an honest look.

Aggressive	Disbeliever	Ms. Popularity	Skulker
Arrogant	Goody-goody	Passive	Smirker
Blamer	Heckler	Pig-headed	Sulky
Bored	Inferior	Pleaser	Superior
Braggart	Know-it-all	Pouter	Trickster
Chameleon	Loudmouth	Procrastinator	Whiner
Cheater	Luckless	Refuser	Worrier
Deflector	Martyr	Shy Guy	

Emoji's showing insecure and secure expressions. Easy to see the difference, isn't it?!

Understanding Thought

For the purpose of Lee's story it is helpful to understand the principle of *Thought* and its impact on feelings. "All feelings derive, and become alive, whether negative or positive, from the power of *Thought*." (Mis. 25) Thought and feeling are intricately related. Simply put, what you think determines what you feel.

As the quality of our thinking diminishes with negative thoughts, we get lower quality feelings such as "hate, jealousy, insecurity, phobias and feelings of depression." As thinking improves with positive thoughts, our feelings such as "compassion, humility, love, joy, happiness and contentment" follow suit. (Mis. 24)

The answer we are looking for isn't in the content or details of a thought, "but in the realization that *Thought* is the common denominator." (Mis. 63) All human experience stems from our thinking. For example, Lee's thinking led to feelings of insecurity. Then new insights guided him to healthy feelings and he could relax into being himself. Once you see a mask of insecurity, like Lee did, you can choose to stop feeding an insecure feeling and regain your security.

- ➢ **Think, pair, share**

Some people spend a lot of time wearing masks and aren't very nice or fun to be around. Actually, none of us are really any of these caricatures. People innocently create disguises. Like any feeling, insecurity is caused only by our thinking. Just knowing insecure thoughts are temporary makes a big difference.

- Have you noticed what people do to feel better when they are insecure? Do they ever end up feeling worse?
- Feelings "become alive, whether positive or negative, from the power of *Thought*." (Mis. 25) You have free will to choose which thoughts to feed. Consider the thoughts you are "feeding" now. Where do they put you on the "security index"? Is your security barely visible or strongly evident, or somewhere in between?

Teen Reflections: How do these reflections resonate with you?

"Your negative thoughts cause you to feel bad and insecure. When you think positive thoughts, you will feel better. Disguises of insecurity are the masks that we put on when we are feeling uneasy about a certain situation. Different people wear different disguises. Learning Three Principles has helped me be more secure about myself and my relationships. Thank you very much!"

"The most valuable is learning more about the power of *Thought* and how moods work. I can use this information in my life. It's made a difference because I look and I understand my negative thoughts work against me to put me in bad moods. Knowing this, I believe, is half the battle for me to be happy, excited, and content in my outside life."

Self-Determination
"Everything is a circle and a circle
naturally has no beginning and no end. ...
The center of this wheel is your free will
and from the center of this wheel
you can go anywhere you want because
that's your free will." (Gre.S. 9:36)

Color of Moods

A mood is simply a state of mind produced by our thoughts in the moment.
Moods in a way are simply a cluster of shifting thoughts.
We can naturally move in and out of moods without effort. It's life!
There's an ebb and flow which means we do have innocent ups and downs.
"Many people make the mistake of believing that their moods create their thoughts;
in reality, it is their thoughts that produce their moods." (Mis. 58)

You create your mood by choosing which thoughts get your attention
just like selecting sunglasses to color the world you see.
Do you see this as true for you?
For example, you can choose thoughts that have you …
~feeling green with envy,
~seeing red and feeling angry or
~feeling sad and blue.

You may choose the rosy hue of an optimistic mood!

My Guide Inside® (Learner Book III)

MGI Chapter Resource Center

Use the resources, activities and projects provided to enhance your learning.
- **Activities**: These are for credit, grades and creativity. Use the criteria for success!
- **Just for Fun**: Enjoy a good feeling.
- **Vital Vocabulary**: Enhance communication.
- **Experiment**: Try this during the week.
- **Appendix D**: "Reminders" deepen understanding.
- **Resources Tab**: myguideinside.com includes Video On Demand to bring this chapter to life, Video Clips that enhance, and Digital Media Options for each activity. Password: mgi

Activities

❖ **Reflect and Write a Journal Entry**
- Write a reflection or respond to one of these ideas; include Vital Vocabulary words.

"The actuality of thought is life." (Aristotle)

"No one can give away wisdom. A teacher can only lead you to it via words, hoping you will have the courage to look within yourself." (Mis. 128)

Success Criteria: : use "I", share thoughts, feelings; show insight, connections.

❖ **Respond to a Video Clip**
- Respond in your journal.

See Resources tab.

Success criteria: use "I," express your ideas clearly; show insight, connections.

❖ **Summarize**
- Create a summary of Lee's story, typically about one third of the original length.

Success criteria: main idea clearly stated, only important details, logical sequence, specific conclusion and correct conventions.

❖ **Create a Work of Art**
- Visually depict both positive and negative thinking. Compare and contrast: A vehicle traveling along smoothly representing "life filled with positive thoughts" and a second vehicle stuck in the muck representing "life filled with negative thoughts."

Success criteria: be original and creative, show skillful use of materials, be expressive and detailed, and use space effectively.

Just for Fun

✓ **Enjoy a Video Clip**
  Living in the Moment Song by Jason Mraz. (Length 3:57)
✓ **ID Faces** … Look back at the emoji faces. How many can you identify?

Vital Vocabulary

Some of these words are relatively simple.
Understanding them in a deeper way will enhance your communication.

Caricature—comically exaggerated representation
Contentment—happiness and satisfaction
Courage—quality of facing challenges directly
Depression—state caused by lack of hope
Derive from—stem from
Disguise—conceal, hide
Element—principle, foundation for a chain of reasoning
Humility—unassuming view of one's abilities
Insecurity—negative feeling that has no fixed form
Jealousy—bitterness, envy
Light-hearted—carefree
Mood—state of mind caused by my thinking in the moment
Optimistic—hopeful
Personae—mask
Phobia—extreme fear
Self-determination— free will
Spiritual—inner

Experiment

All Those Millions! What if you were left millions by some long lost relative? In order to get the money, you must be in a good mood for three days. You wear a monitoring device that records any negative feelings such as anger, fear, boredom, frustration, and more. If you dip into these there will be a warning to change quickly or lose the money. You must also keep up your regular routine. Have fun with this idea. It shows that we have more choice regarding our feelings than we may initially think!

Chapter 3
Flawsome and Fun: Our True Identity

Who and what we are inside is what counts! With one big insight, supermodel Tyra Banks coined the term "flawsome"—awesome even with flaws—when she was publicly criticized for not being physically perfect.

We all have a tendency to hold on to critical thoughts about our identity. We can be our own worst critics. Consider how focusing on faults and judging yourself leads to unhappiness. Have you noticed that when you are contented you are not busy judging yourself or anyone else? Judgment is only a thought; if you allow such personal thinking to pass, you will see with clarity; then it is easy to accept that, like everyone, you are "flawsome." Athletes are also using this knowledge to be "in the zone."

There is logical cause and effect at play: negative thoughts produce negative feelings and positive thoughts create positive feelings. Free will means it's your choice which thoughts receive your attention. There is comic relief in discovering it is all in your head. For example, you may think everyone is watching you but so often, like everyone else, you just perceive an audience. One teen shares: "I experience insights all the time—big and small. I see things closer to how they really are, which is just so cool. It makes you feel so happy and so free. I cherish moments like this, where I really see with no filter. I find moments like [these] to be worth all the craziness."

This chapter deepens understanding of the principles by drawing out your inner wisdom and pointing to your true identity. Focus is on the logical cause effect relationship of personal thinking to feeling, and your power to choose to hold on to or let go of a thought.

Gina's Story
Connect what is read with how you see your own identity.

Gina had a reputation for looking really great. Since middle school, her appearance had been very important and she worked hard on it. She'd designed a complex beauty and fitness routine, and even though she was already seen as especially attractive by her peers, she felt a strong need to push through her regimen every day. She did this even when it created pressure, or when she could have thought of better things to do.

Gina felt confused. Sometimes she wanted to be more relaxed so she could fit in and have good friends. When she was at home, she was besieged by nagging thoughts to keep trying to improve her "look." It was as if nothing else was as important, as if her appearance alone determined her identity in life.

As Gina started her afternoon work-out, she felt her face getting hot-- but not from the exercise. She remembered an embarrassing incident from earlier that day. Kaylee, a girl she hardly knew, had complimented her on how "in shape" she looked. Rather than thanking her, Gina had begun complaining about her "imperfect" hips. "I work so hard, and it barely makes a difference."

"Your hips?" Kaylee exclaimed. "Oh, come on! Just look at mine!" Still feeling dissatisfied, Gina replied, "Your hips are fine for you!" Kaylee's eyes widened. "You mean my imperfect hips match the rest of my imperfect self?" Before Gina could speak, Kaylee stormed off.

Remembering the event, Gina wished she could feel content and be more easy-going. There were so many things she could have said to Kaylee instead of complaining and sounding so negative. Her thoughts trailed off as she concentrated on what she was doing. She was relieved when her phone rang; her heart wasn't into exercising today.

Gina got off the phone in a totally different mood. She was thrilled! She had a date! Dates were rare for Gina because although she didn't realize it, guys saw her as unapproachable or "out of their league." The date was with Steve, a friend of her cousin Rosalie's. She had met him at a family gathering a few years ago.

Steve was in town as the coach of a swim team and had free time. Gina thought wistfully about the fun she'd had that summer with him and her cousin. Life was so simple then! They agreed to meet at the beach the next day. They'd go swimming and have a bite to eat at one of the cafes.

∞

Gina spotted Steve immediately. She felt a little shy walking toward him, but he bounded over and gave her a big hug. She was delighted with how at ease Steve was. They fell into a comfortable, open-ended conversation. Steve seemed genuinely interested in how her life was going. His face lit up telling her how great "his" kids on the swim team were despite funny stories of their mischievous antics.

"I can laugh about it now, but for a while I was really stressed about them not being serious enough. It wasn't until this season's coaching clinics started that I realized I was letting my thoughts about losing meets take the fun out of the whole thing—not just for me, but for the kids, too."

Gina was intrigued and asked to hear more. "What happened at the clinics to change your attitude?"

"We learned about Three Principles that work together to create our experience of life.

Everyone has an inner compass guiding us toward using those principles wisely. When I realized I was using the principle of *Thought* to create a stressful feeling for myself and our team, my perspective changed. My stressful thoughts fell away and I started enjoying everything much more. And the kids actually settled down and did better in competition once I lightened up."

Steve recalled a passage from one of the coaching clinic books: "When you start to see the power of *Thought* and its relationship to your way of observing life, you will better understand yourself and the world in which you live." (Mis. 52)

He noted, "I didn't realize how much I'd been judging my own faults, which led to major discontent. We talked through a lot of examples during the clinics. I discovered I had a tendency to compare myself with others, trying to become some amazing coach whose team never lost a meet."

"Whoa, that's a lot to live up to!" Gina laughed.

"You're telling me! But you know, I was surprised to learn that it's not unusual for people to become prisoners of their own thoughts. Once you see it, though, the solution is simple."

"Hmmmm…" Gina replied.

Steve was discovering the well-being that is naturally inside each of us. He explained, "You don't have to work at it; listening to your inner voice is key. Now I'm seeing what being in the zone really means!" Gina loved the light-hearted way Steve talked about his learning.

After a stop in the changing room, Gina headed toward the water, her thoughts again focused on how she looked. She felt a little uncomfortable thinking others were admiring her, yet walked for her "audience."

Steve was waiting at the shore. It was fun being with him at the beach and he had some good body surfing tips. Gina caught a few good waves, no problem. She thought she was on a roll!

Unfortunately, before she knew it, she was IN the wave. The rushing water tossed her about so much she had no idea which way was up. She panicked, imagining everyone on the shore looking at her, and grabbed her suit with both hands. At that moment, she felt her face crunching into the sand and shells as the wave washed over her and rolled back out to sea.

Gina was humiliated. Her face was burning and she was mad at herself for worrying how she looked instead of protecting herself as Steve had instructed. He ran to help her and was kind and empathetic, but could not help laughing a little at the sight of her sand encrusted face. Gina was in pain, but she found Steve's warmth disarming and started to smile in spite of herself.

Steve said, "Nobody's perfect and now you're flawsome like the rest of us!" Gina shook her head and looked at him

quizzically. "What did you say I am?"

"You know—flawsome. Awesome, even with flaws!" he grinned. "Your face will heal, and anyway," he reassured her, "it's who and what you are inside that counts." As Steve helped clean the sand off Gina's face; she began to relax and realized in surprise that she was feeling better than she had in a long time.

∞

Gina's thinking cleared as she surveyed the sparkling water and the clear blue sky and she had an insight. She saw the logic of how she had been innocently creating problems with all the misguided thoughts about her appearance. She had been preventing her own happiness! She understood what Steve meant about people holding themselves "prisoner" with their thinking. Clearly she really wanted to be good friends with people and have fun, even if that meant laughing at herself, and not "looking her best."

Some months later, Steve and Gina met again at a big family gathering at Rosalie's house. They laughed uproariously about the day she "bit the beach!"

Now that she is more in touch with her true identity— "who and what you are inside," Gina still maintains a beauty and fitness routine, but with far less attention. She knows she's okay and she's happy. She is grateful that her world has opened up, and she really *sees* the people around her, instead of worrying about an "audience" judging her. Others find Gina approachable and friendly. Incidentally, Gina went out of her way to make up with Kaylee, and they have since become great friends.

> **Let's talk about the big picture.**
- The logic of contaminating thoughts holding us "prisoner" is always the same. How is the logic in Gina's story like what you know?
- How does this statement relate to your experience? "Judging your own faults or the faults of others leads to unhappiness. A mind that dwells in non-judgment is a contented mind." (Mis. 118)

Teen Reflections: How does this reflection resonate with you?

"We get ourselves into sticky situations unconsciously and make our lives unnecessarily painful and difficult. Gina's mind cleared and she experienced what was really going on. She naturally felt happy and content. I experience insights like this all the time—big and small. I see things closer to how they really are, which is just so cool. It makes you feel so happy and so free. I cherish moments like this, where I really see with no filter. I find moments like [these] to be worth all of the craziness."

Cause and Effect

Cause and effect reasoning applies to everyone. When Gina judged herself, she felt dissatisfied. "When our mind is filled with negative thoughts, cause and effect rule, creating a negative feeling." When Gina discovered her natural true identity, she felt content, even happy. "When our mind is filled with positive thoughts, cause and effect rule, resulting in a positive feeling." (Mis. 111)

"Once you become *grateful*, the prison bars of your mind will fall away. Peace of mind and contentment will be yours." (Mis. 131)

MGI Chapter Resource Center

Use the resources, activities and projects provided to enhance your learning.
- **Activities**: These are for credit, grades and creativity. Use the criteria for success!
- **Just for Fun**: Enjoy a good feeling.
- **Vital Vocabulary**: Enhance communication.
- **Experiment**: Try this during the week.
- **Appendix D**: "Reminders" deepen understanding.
- **Resources Tab**: myguideinside.com includes Video On Demand to bring this chapter to life, Video Clips that enhance, and Digital Media Options for each activity. Password: mgi

Activities

❖ **Reflect and Write a Journal Entry**
- Write a reflection or respond to one of these ideas; include Vital Vocabulary words.

"Judging your own faults or the faults of others leads to unhappiness. A mind that dwells in non-judgment is a contented mind." (Mis. 118)

"Life's too important to be taken seriously." (Oscar Wilde)

Success Criteria: use "I," share thoughts, feelings; show insight, connections.

❖ **Respond to a Video Clip**
- Respond in your journal.

See Resources tab.

Success criteria: use "I," express your ideas clearly; show insight, connections.

❖ **Create a Listicle**
- Five Ways to Spend Time without Judging Myself

Discuss five healthy experiences where you do not judge yourself. Reflect on options and new healthy opportunities; there are so many things for you to try, some for the first time. Write a paragraph and include an image for each of the five examples. Include a strong, possibly humorous, last line.

Success criteria: be original, clearly express ideas and include images to reinforce text. Use correct conventions, include a strong last line.

❖ **Update Profile Page**
- Update Gina's profile page now that she is no longer a prisoner of her own thinking about appearance. In a paragraph, include two or three ideas for each: status update, friends, major events and favorites.

Success criteria: engaging voice is evident, unique and clear language with correct conventions.

❖ **Create a Work of Art**
- Draw a picture of anything you personally see in this story. It can be anything. What occurs to you? Or create a picture of something opening … a cage, door, flower, book or anything to symbolize freeing yourself from being a prisoner of contaminated thoughts.

Success criteria: be original and creative, show skillful use of materials, be expressive and detailed. Use space effectively.

Just for Fun

✓ **Enjoy a Video Clip …**
Everything is Sound Song by Jason Mraz. (Length 4:46)

✓ **Create a Friend Advisory …** Create two "friend advisories" for Gina: one for the start of the story and one for the end of the story.
Friend Advisory: 3 Good, 2 Average, 1 Poor. Did you see any change?

Rate Gina at the beginning of the story:

| Honest | 3 2 1 | Likable | 3 2 1 | Supportive | 3 2 1 |
| Kind | 3 2 1 | Fair | 3 2 1 | Optimistic | 3 2 1 |

Rate Gina at the end of the story:

| Honest | 3 2 1 | Likable | 3 2 1 | Supportive | 3 2 1 |
| Kind | 3 2 1 | Fair | 3 2 1 | Optimistic | 3 2 1 |

How do you rate your own "friendliness"? Remember we continuously develop!

✓ **Overthinking, anyone? …** We all frequently tend to focus on ourselves too much. We think about who we are, who we think we should be, what others think of us, and we think about who we think others think we should be. Is it a struggle just to read this? This personal habit of overthinking leads to confusion and unhappiness. But there is a way out! Like Gina, you can experience a naturally clear mind. Mental clarity leads to a positive feeling. There is nothing you need to do; this knowing and happiness is inside you all the time.

✓ **Comic Relief …** Go for humor; write about an imaginary character with an inflated view of self. Then complete this sentence about the imaginary person, "Fortunately, ___." Crumple your paper into a snowball. Toss it to someone else in the group. Catch another ball and smooth out that paper. Complete this sentence "Unfortunately, ___." Repeat this process. Finally, take turns reading the group compositions aloud. How are not understanding the power of *Thought* and this snowball activity alike?

Vital Vocabulary
Some of these words are relatively simple.
Understanding them in a deeper way will enhance your communication.

Cause—reason
Contaminated—something made impure
Content—satisfied
Delusion—false impression
Disarming—allaying suspicion
Effect—result
Empathy—ability to understand feelings of others
Fairness—justness and sensitivity to needs of others
Flawsome—awesome even with flaws
Humiliate—injure someone's dignity
Logic—used to anticipate results of actions
Misguided—showing faulty judgment or reasoning
Negative—bad, not wanted
Positive—good, useful
Pressure—stressful urgency
Self-image—the idea one has of one's self
Self-importance—an exaggerated sense of one's own importance

Experiment

Explore the logic of the cause and effect rule for yourself! In your own life notice when you experience negative thoughts creating negative feelings or positive thoughts creating positive feelings. Throughout the week, notice what insights you have during this experiment.

Chapter 4
Living in the Present:
Leaving the Past in the Dust

Many individuals have a rough start in life due to circumstances beyond their control. They may feel confused and angry, thinking they have no other choice. "That is just how life will always be for me." Have you ever been treated with empathy and compassion? What happened?

A caring relationship can open a "chink in the armor" of even the most hardened teens who live with fear and distrust. Just a tiny opening prepares anyone for an insight about the beauty of their true self which is always healthy and undamaged. Those who have lived through hard times and catch this new view of themselves are free and grateful. They find inner wisdom and inevitably become powerful examples and mentors to others.

Our guide inside helps us all see life from a neutral, secure perspective filled with wisdom and joy. A teen says, "We don't have the power to choose the life that we are born into, but we do have the power to create our experience of it. … Life is a piano … You get to write your own music. Your thoughts create your life story. You are the composer. Pick your notes wisely!"

This chapter stresses that we have the natural human ability for intuition and insights, which increase personal well-being. Focus is on discovering that difficult circumstances do not determine life experience and that caring relationships may foster life-changing insights in others.

Lenny's Story
©Jane Tucker, 1999, Middletown, MD (adapted 2016)
Visualize images to gain understanding.

Angry shouts blasted through the thin bedroom wall, followed by slurred sarcasm and yelling. Lenny was jolted from a deep dream.

"Shut up," he thought fiercely. "Shut up! Stop it!"

Lenny felt the bed shaking, and turned to his little brother beside him. His skinny arms clasped a pillow tightly over his ears and his small body trembled with sobs.

"Josh, it's okay." Lenny reached over and rubbed his brother's back. "It's okay," he repeated. Josh squirmed over to him, one arm still trying to block out the sound with his pillow, and buried his face in Lenny's chest. Both boys tensed at each new shout, at each crash of something being thrown and broken. They held onto each other until the front door finally slammed. It was nearly dawn before Lenny got back to sleep.

The next school day was like all the others. Lenny felt the teachers glaring at him, looking for any excuse to bust him down to the principal's office. He had no interest in the stupid subjects they were trying to cram down his throat. None of it had anything to do with real life.

The other kids got on his nerves; some intentionally annoyed him. He hated the popular group, teacher's pets and snobs who made fun of him or put him down. Everyone discovered how dangerous it was to mess with Lenny. He'd been suspended twice for fighting. He'd been glad to get the two weeks off—it was almost worth the punishing beatings he got at home because of it. People were afraid of him now and he thought that was good.

∞

As the years passed, things got worse. By the time Lenny turned sixteen, his father was gone. His mother Cora said, "Good riddance to bad rubbish." She felt his father, Vince, had never been an asset to the family. She was the one who worked long hours waiting tables to pay the rent and put food on the table. She was worn out, married to a man who cared more about the bottle than about her, and she was bringing up two boys with no support.

Cora hated yelling at Lenny and Josh so much, but she didn't know what else to do. The big one was always getting kicked out of school, failing every subject, and mean as a rat. The only one he ever showed any kindness toward was his little brother. And that one! If Lenny was a rat, Josh was a mole. Always sullen looking, so quiet one teacher had sent a note home asking if he was mute. He didn't get in trouble at school like Lenny did, but he was barely passing. Neither ever helped around the house unless she threatened repeatedly. Some nights she just cried herself to sleep, then berated herself in the morning for being so weak.

One afternoon at work, Cora received an emergency phone call. The police had Lenny in custody. As soon as her shift finished, she rushed to the station. Looking at her son shackled and in handcuffs, she heard the story.

On the way home, Lenny had seen a bigger boy picking on Josh, pushing and calling him names. Lenny jumped on the kid, knocked him down, and began punching his face. According to witnesses, Lenny seemed out of control, almost out of his mind. He started choking the boy, and didn't stop even when the victim lost consciousness.

Thankfully the school's football coach saw what was going on and stopped his car. He pulled Lenny back, restrained him, and called the police.

At the hearing Cora was torn between grief, shame and relief as Lenny was sent away. Riding home on the bus, Josh sat like a stone beside his mother.

∞

Lenny opened his eyes and stared at the cracked ceiling tiles in his shared cell at the detention center. His back ached from springs poking through the lumpy mattress. He heard his bunkmate below snoring, and guys in the other bunks breathing and wheezing.

Gazing up at the dingy grayness, Lenny felt nothing. He was where everyone had told him he'd end up—no surprise. Something was gnawing away in the pit of his stomach, but he refused to acknowledge it. Instinctively he knew fear was not allowed in this place—to show it would invite cruelty. He closed his eyes and hoped Josh would be alright without him.

The first few weeks were an intense boot camp with drills every day, hard physical labor, and constant humiliation by aggressive, yelling officers. Lenny was numb. He learned early that talking back brought swift, harsh punishment, so he deadened his impulses. He felt sick all the time. Outwardly, he was adjusting to the program but inwardly he was seething with anger and thoughts of revenge.

At this time the juvenile justice system in Lenny's state changed. Lenny's camp was shut down and he was shipped to a new rural center.

∞

Two youths slept in each room, and they had a window. Activities were held at a more moderate pace; chores were less punishing. The staff members used reason rather than force and intimidation; the atmosphere was less tense. Lenny didn't need to watch his back as much.

At this center, residents had a choice of regular school classes during the day, or daytime chores and evenings working with tutors to study for the high school equivalency (GED) exam. Lenny hated school, so the idea of taking an exam instead of going to classes appealed to him. Walking back to his cottage from the study building at night, he saw for the first time the vastness of dark, endless skies filled with thousands of shining stars.

Each day, he was required to work outside—digging garden beds, planting seeds, hoeing, pulling weeds. When his seeds began to poke through the ground, he felt an unexpected sense of excitement.

Every once in a while, as he worked with his hands in the earth, warm sun on his back and breezes cooling his skin, the tight knot in Lenny's stomach loosened a little. He caught a glimpse of something he hardly recognized—a feeling of peace. He thought about Josh and wished he could share the feeling with him.

After a month, Lenny was required to attend bi-weekly group meetings with a counselor named Angela. He didn't know what to make of her. She seemed too sunny, too happy. He figured she must be older than him, but not by much. The way she talked and acted, she was either totally ignorant or completely fake. There was no way in this world she was going to teach him anything.

Arms folded tight across his chest, Lenny leaned his chair against the far wall with his long legs stretched out to balance his weight. His eyes were slits as he watched the other boys in a circle playing some stupid game … something to do with guessing parts of songs, choosing favorite music groups. He deliberately blocked out Angela's voice when she gave instructions. He had no idea what everybody was laughing about.

After the game ended and the laughing subsided, Angela read from a little book and the boys quieted down, "Our thoughts are the camera, our eyes are the lens. Put them together and the picture we see is reality." (Mis. 55)

These words just confused Lenny. "More games," he said to himself, and tuned out. When the group broke up, he rose and headed straight for the door.

"Lenny," Angela called to him. He stopped, but didn't turn around. She came up beside him, touched his arm and gave him a copy of the book she'd been reading, *The Missing Link*, by Sydney Banks. "Thanks for coming."

"As if I had a choice," Lenny thought to himself.

The book lay unopened on the small table beside his bed for several days. Then one night, he picked it up and started to read. He was tired from working outdoors and perhaps that allowed something to get through. A feeling came over him as he read. Although he couldn't really remember feeling like this before, it was somehow familiar and comforting. He was drawn to read a few pages every night; it always helped him sleep.

The next week Lenny walked into the group half an hour late. The boys were laughing as they concluded another one of Angela's games. He fully expected to be in big trouble, but Angela didn't even seem to notice. Instead of reading him the riot act, she just smiled and said "Hi, Lenny."

∞

This time, Lenny didn't feel the need to park his chair against the wall. He sat back, just outside the circle, and observed. He listened to Angela reading from *The Missing Link*. He was surprised the same strong feeling he'd been experiencing from reading it on his own seemed to fill the room. It was almost spooky because there was such peace. Angela continued:

"Your thoughts are like the artist's brush. They create a *personal* picture of the reality you live in.
Thought, like the rudder of a ship, steers us to the safety of open waters or the doom of rocky shores."

(Mis. 56)

Something struck Lenny. A new feeling brought him to tears. Perhaps he wasn't fated to the doom of rocky shores forever. He didn't completely understand what it all meant, but somehow, for the first time he felt a glimmer of hope.

As members of the group talked, Lenny could hardly believe his ears. They were saying things he'd never heard any kids say before. These were guys like him, guys who usually talked tough. But this big, rough looking kid told everyone he felt forgiveness for people he used to hate!

Angela said something about everyone being psychologically innocent—they had been doing the best they knew how to do, given how they saw life. There was just something they had not had a chance to discover yet. Lenny shook his head and thought, "Come on! If they were innocent, what were they all doing locked up?" This whole thing was making no sense. But yet …

Something about the feeling in the room touched Lenny. He noticed kids from rival gangs talking together and laughing like friends. He felt Angela looked at him in a way no one ever had, except for Josh. It was a look of pure acceptance with no judgment.

Gradually Lenny became more involved. He actually started looking forward to meetings and he was developing friendships that made his days less lonely; he had fun kicking the soccer ball or shooting hoops. He realized that, aside from Josh, he'd never in his life had a real friend. His world had been competition, fighting, and self-protection. Now, somehow, he was beginning to let his guard down, and it felt strange, but good.

At one of the meetings, a boy named Ty started listing everyone who was to blame for his being there. He described how his family had let him down, so-called friends had used him, and all his teachers had been out to get him. The boy's voice became more and more bitter and angry. When he finished, there was a pause.

Then, very gently, Angela asked, "Ty, is anyone hurting you, right now?"

The boy looked startled. Slowly, he answered, "No."

She gazed at him with nothing but kindness and his face started to relax.

The counselor went on, "It's so easy to blame. But do you know what focusing on blame does to us? Think about it."

After a silence, Ty admitted, "Keeps you feeling lousy."

She leaned forward toward him. "You've got it! As long as we do that, we're giving away control of our lives to other people, to circumstances, to the past. Blame is just a thought that keeps us from our happiness."

Lenny had never heard such an idea before. For the next few days, it kept coming back to him. He started to notice the burden of blame he carried toward his mother, father, teachers, peers, and especially toward himself.

At the end of the day, lying in his bunk, he again opened *The Missing Link*. These words felt like they'd been written just for him, just for this moment in his life.

"When you learn to forgive those who have wronged you in the past,
you clear your mind and bring harmony into your life,
allowing you to see what *is*,
instead of what *isn't*.

What isn't … *is life seen through distorted memories.*
What is … *is life seen as it truly is now, clear of all falsehoods.*" (Mis. 112)

The words resonated, touching him somewhere deep inside and he drifted off to sleep. Lenny woke feeling oddly refreshed. The sun streamed in his window, birds sang, and the thought of working in the garden filled him with pleasure. He imagined how shocked his mother would be if she could see him now, actually looking forward to doing a chore. Lenny realized he had just thought of his mother with affection. "Incredible!"

Suddenly, the words he'd read and Angela had said made sense. His life-long awful feelings of blame and hatred weren't set in stone. His feelings shifted and he relaxed into a peaceful state. He discovered he could bring back old feelings with his thinking, but he didn't want to. For the first time, Lenny saw he had a choice.

In the days ahead, Lenny had moments of deep happiness and compassion. His former constant companion, anger, reared its ugly head less often. He effortlessly enjoyed helping others rather than hurting them. In the group meetings, he started sharing how his life was changing. He was amazed when others were deeply affected by his words. They were actually happy for him. Angela kept bringing their conversations back to the principle of *Thought*—saying, "It's so natural. As our thoughts naturally become more positive, our lives become nicer."

Lenny emerged as a peacemaker, defusing fights with laughter and common sense. Sometimes when he thought of the first detention center, it seemed like someone else's life.

He was now so grateful. What had begun as harsh punishment became a gift. At his release staff members could see his true rehabilitation.

∞

Back home Lenny was surprised by very different feelings about everything. He still felt strong affection for his brother, but it was more relaxed; he did not worry about Josh. In the past their conversations had been all about how unfair life was. They complained and plotted revenge. Now, when Josh said a kid was mean to him, Lenny explained when people were mean, they were really miserable, lost in their own negative, fearful thoughts.

"I ought to know!" he laughed. "If you see where someone's coming from, you don't take it personally and it doesn't bother you. Even teachers—they're just doing the best they can, depending on what they think is going on. I know it's true. I can't believe I'm saying this—remember how I hated all the teachers?"

Lenny wasn't taking Josh's side anymore but sharing what he knew. Josh felt better each time they talked. Josh saw how his own thinking created his experience in each moment. His confidence grew, grades improved, and he laughed more.

Cora had been skeptical of the detention center's glowing reports. She kept waiting for Lenny to fall back into a bad attitude. Still, she couldn't deny he was much more co-operative and helpful. Josh was following Lenny's lead! If Lenny got angry, it was very short-lived, and he was quick to apologize. Cora even found herself apologizing to him after an argument. That was a first! When Lenny passed the GED exam, got a full-time job, and started contributing financially, Cora finally understood that this was not an act. Her son had really changed, and their family was much calmer, even happy.

Lenny's father started dropping by to see the boys on weekends. After the first couple of visits Vince made a point of arriving clearheaded. Touched by the unconditional love of his sons he felt better about himself.

He teared up realizing he was forgiven for his mistakes and had another chance to be a dad.

After a year of steady employment and regular visits with the family that were night and day different from the interactions they used to have, Vince asked his wife if she would take him back. Because of Lenny, Cora was able to understand anyone can change. Gratefulness replaced her bitterness, and she knew this man was no longer the person he had been. They reconciled, and the past was truly left behind. Something greater than any of them, but present within all of them, guided the family into a future full of promise.

Lenny learned a powerful lesson. He discovered people can, regardless of past circumstances, indeed move beyond very difficult life events. The key is realizing that you have a choice: either holding on to old thinking and keeping past hurts alive, or being open to an insight that delivers a new perspective. During group, without intentionally doing anything, Lenny had begun to settle down. He noticed he was beginning to feel whole and healthy. The more he read and listened, the more he was naturally self-regulating. As time passed he noticed something new, something he had been missing. Lenny discovered the battle was over. He could see these principles are true for everyone. In his own way and with his own words, he naturally began sharing what he knew with his brother. Lenny was grateful to no longer be in trouble. He was rid of negative thoughts and anger, and filled with hope. Simply stated, this shift was the start of his happy life.

> ➤ **Let's talk about the big picture.**
> - Lenny's story may or may not relate to your experience, but the logic of choice—holding on to old thinking or being open to an insight—is always the same. How is the logic in this story like something you know?
>   - What was that "something" guiding Lenny's family?

>   - We have all been in trouble at one time or another, and probably felt maltreated. Everyone has history others do not see. No matter how different you think you are — we are all equal. It is best to be yourself; "everyone else is already taken." (Oscar Wilde) Talk about what this means: "Never, never, never put yourself down. There is nobody … that is any better or any worse than you. And if you can see that, that's where you find pride, and joy, and just a loving life. You just become neutral." (One 7:12)

Teen Reflection: How does it resonate with you?
"We don't have the power to choose the life that we are born into, but we do have the power to create our experience of it. We cannot blame circumstances, although it is easy to believe "something out there" is causing you to feel terrible. When you realize all of your feelings are coming from your own thinking, there is a sense of peace, freedom, and empowerment.

Life is a piano: your thoughts are your fingers; you hear and experience only the notes you choose to play. You are not forced by circumstance to feel a certain way or play one note. A piano has 88 keys. You get to write your own music. Your thoughts create your life story. You are the composer. Pick your notes wisely!"

Find "a grateful feeling for what you already have in life." (Mis. 130)

MGI Chapter Resource Center

Use the resources, activities and projects provided to enhance your learning.
- **Activities**: These are for credit, grades and creativity. Use the criteria for success!
- **Just for Fun**: Enjoy a good feeling.
- **Vital Vocabulary**: Enhance communication.
- **Experiment**: Try this during the week.
- **Appendix D**: "Reminders" deepen understanding.
- **Resources Tab**: myguideinside.com includes Video On Demand to bring this chapter to life, Video Clips that enhance, and Digital Media Options for each activity. Password: mgi

Activities

❖ **Reflect and Write a Journal Entry**
- Write a reflection or respond to one of these ideas; include Vital Vocabulary words.

"May the stars carry your sadness away, may the flowers fill your heart with beauty, may hope forever wipe away your tears." (Chief Dan George)

"Never, never, never put yourself down. There is nobody … that is any better or any worse than you. And if you can see that, that's where you find pride, and joy, and just a loving life. You just become neutral." (One 7:12)

You may also consider offering your responses to *The Secret*: Mavis Karn's letter found at the end of this chapter.

Success Criteria: use "I," share thoughts, feelings; show insight, connections.

❖ **Respond to a Video Clip**
- Respond in your journal.

See Resources tab.

Success Criteria: use "I," express your ideas clearly; show insight, connections.

❖ **Add to the Story**
- The story is a timeline for Lenny. Consider two scenarios:

– Scenario A: Suppose Lenny did not learn Three Principles. List a few descriptors of how his life turns out a year from now.
– Scenario B: Consider his insight that he wasn't fated to the "doom of rocky shores" forever and that he began feeling hopeful about his life.

Write about what's happening for Lenny a year from now. Include something fantastic that he never previously thought was possible. Write a conclusion statement about the power of *Thought* in these two scenarios.

Success Criteria: focused central idea, meaningful text shows depth of thought and logical sequence. Use clear language and correct conventions. Make your writer's voice engaging.

- ❖ **Write a Poem**
  - Read "The Ultimate Surprise" prize winning poem as an example; it's found at the end of this chapter.
  - Write a poem about the power of *Thought* or describing the story of a specific thought you have had. Create an entirely original poem or use one of these sample starts:
  - Choose to use the power of *Thought* to …
  - A thought is like a seed …
  - A thought alone has no life of its own …

  Publish your poem for others to enjoy.

  Success Criteria: show depth of thought, be organized, use vivid language and create a mood.

- ❖ **Create a Work of Art**
  - See the example illustration for "The Ultimate Surprise" found at the end of this chapter.
  - Illustrate the poem you wrote and add a title.

  Success Criteria: be original and creative, show skillful use of materials, be expressive and detailed. Use space effectively.

- ❖ **Recite a Poem**

  Memorize your poem and present it to the group.

  Success Criteria: be prepared and accurate, speak clearly and be confident.

Just for Fun

- ✓ **Create a Friend Advisory …** Create two "friend advisories" for Lenny: one for the start of the story and one for the end of the story.

  Friend Advisory: 3 Good, 2 Average, 1 Poor. Did you see any change?

Rate Lenny at the beginning of the story:

| Honest | 3 2 1 | Likable | 3 2 1 | Supportive | 3 2 1 |
| Kind | 3 2 1 | Fair | 3 2 1 | Optimistic | 3 2 1 |

Rate Lenny at the end of the story:

| Honest | 3 2 1 | Likable | 3 2 1 | Supportive | 3 2 1 |
| Kind | 3 2 1 | Fair | 3 2 1 | Optimistic | 3 2 1 |

- ✓ **Thought Fires** … How do you know a bonfire is dying down? What happens if you add more firewood for fuel? How is this like your thinking? What happens when you stop adding mental fuel, when you stop focusing on a certain thought? Does a thought alone have a life of its own?
- ✓ **Memory Name Game** … Say your name, add a verb starting with the same letter as your name; create a sentence. Example: Hugh hides the treats in the fridge. Next person adds their name sentence, and repeats all the other sentences in order. When the group finishes how does your head feel? Move beyond the activity; let all those memories go. What does your head feel like now? How is this applicable to your daily life?

Vital Vocabulary
Some of these words are relatively simple.
Understanding them in a deeper way will enhance your communication.

Acceptance—the act of accepting with approval; favorable reception
Circumstances—life events or conditions
Distorted—misleading, untrue
Empowerment—becoming strong and more confident
Grateful—thankful, appreciative of the goodness of life
Harmony—agreement, understanding, co-operation
Initiative—self-motivation
Judgment—opinion, conclusion or evaluation
Neutral—fair and unbiased, neither positive nor negative
Psychologically—pertaining to mental functioning
Rehabilitation—making a positive turnaround in life
Self-regulate—ability to stay calmly focused
Skeptical—having doubts

Experiment

Explore the great outdoors regularly. Get your mind off yourself and see what newness appears in your life. Consider sharing your experience with the class, a friend or family member.

The Ultimate Surprise

A fountain of waves
the blowing of the wind
everywhere yet nowhere
a constant all the same

The opening and closing
an unknown from which we came
everything we ever see
yet illusive all the same

Difference is the outcome
Unity is before
Harmony is the birthright
of which we see no more

Learn to listen freely
without a busy mind
it's in the quiet chambers
where peace and truth is found

It's right before your very eyes
yet not directly in front
Look behind and you will find
the everywhere yet nowhere…
the ultimate surprise

©2016 Paul Lock and Paul Lock Art. Surrey, UK. Printed with special permission.

A seasoned Minnesota social worker in private practice, Mavis, volunteered to facilitate a Three Principles group for young men in a juvenile detention facility. She and Willie, a friend and colleague half her age, drove two hours each way on Sundays, to share the principles with a group very much like Lenny's.

At first the group was very hostile. The young men were amazed Willie and Mavis even came back. Change happened. Mavis wrote this letter as a gift given to each member at the last session. The group secretly had ordered a cake and it was a joyous, hopeful celebration inside the detention center. This letter has been shared far and wide over the years!

THE SECRET   by Mavis Karn, LSW (See 4 min video in the OL resources)

Dear Kids (and former kids),

I have a secret to tell you. Nobody meant to keep it from you… it's just that it's been one of those things that's so obvious that people couldn't see it … like looking all over for the key that you have in your hand.

The secret is that you are already a completely whole, perfect person. You are not damaged goods, you are not incomplete, you are not flawed, you are not unfinished, you do not need re-modeling, fixing, polishing or major rehabilitation. You already have within you everything you need to live a wonderful life. You have common sense, wisdom, genius, creativity, humor, self-esteem … you are pure potential … you are missing nothing.

The only thing that can keep you from enjoying all that you already are is a thought. One thought. Your thought. Not someone else's thought. Your thought … Whatever thought you are thinking at the moment that feels more important to think than feeling grateful alive, content, joyful, optimistic, loving and at peace … that's the only thing that's between you and happiness.

And guess who's in charge of your thinking … guess who gets to decide where your attention goes… guess who gets to write, produce, direct and star in the moment you're in the middle of… you. Just you. Not your past (stored thought), not the future (did you ever notice that it never, ever shows up?), not your parents (they all think their own thoughts), or your friends (ditto), or school or media or situations or circumstances or anything else. Just you.

Thought is an awesome capability. Like any capability it can be used either as a tool or as a weapon against ourselves and others. And just like with any other tool, we can tell whether we're using it for or against ourselves by how it feels. When we use the power of Thought against ourselves or others, we get in trouble. When we don't, we usually stay out of trouble.

FEELINGS EXIST TO WARN US AWAY FROM USING THOUGHT TO CREATE TROUBLE IN OUR LIVES AND TO GUIDE US BACK TO OUR NATURAL, HEALTHY ABILITY TO LIVE OUR LIVES TO THE FULLEST.

So, … please remember that your thoughts are not always telling you the truth. When we're in low moods, feeling down, our thoughts are not to be trusted … our IQ's drop. When our thoughts pass and we lighten up, our thinking is once again creative, positive … our IQ's go up. The only way you can feel badly about yourself and your life is if you think badly about them … it's up to you, every single minute you're alive. It's always up to you! This is the best, most liberating secret I ever learned, and I want you to know it too. With love, Mavis

© 1999, 2016, Mavis L. Karn. Printed with special permission.

Chapter 5
Understanding the Lost Thinker

*We all have been lost thinkers at times. Sometimes we act like aggressors and in other situations we feel like victims. There is actually only one problem. Everyone occasionally pays attention to misleading thoughts. You may think you or a friend feels social pressures to be a certain way or do something. The solution is to listen to your **Guide Inside**, innate inner wisdom, to gain a more accurate understanding.*

You are part of several groups or mini-cultures. Not every group member may be directly part of a social problem but everyone can be part of the solution. You may not personally be dealing with a difficulty but you may clearly notice someone else is. Your wisdom can help you understand how to support peers who face challenges. No one needs to live in the shadows. You have insights about how to treat someone with encouragement, kindness and dignity. A little support goes a long, long way.

As one teen reflects, "When we relate from a place of caring and understanding instead of anger and retaliation, we give others the opportunity to let go of the negative thought patterns creating their unpleasant lives. This naturally creates a more easy-going world for everyone."

This chapter creates opportunities for you to occasionally see yourself as a "lost thinker" and use common sense and reflection to experience new thinking. This improves communication skills and increases social and digital responsibility.

A Teen's Blog: Thoughts and Ramblings as I Gain Understanding
What questions do you hope I answer in my blog posts?

October: I am on assignment looking for evidence of social and digital responsibility in my world. I am supposed to include some advice for solving problems and building relationships.

I am a regular high school student. I don't really belong to any one group but have a few good friends and hang out with a popular crowd. I moved here three years ago when I was 13. I keep my grades up and am seen as a good person, but I was put behind bars for a few hours for petty theft. Stealing suntan lotion and planning to skip out the next day turned out to be the most humiliating thing. What was I thinking? That's not social responsibility. Well, it doesn't matter; I'm done with that. That's not me.

At school, I find it intriguing that some people have kind of cemented their roles already. There is one guy, Gavin, who is so mean, he goes around being intimidating and getting in the face of anyone he sees as different, whatever that means to him. He always gloats when he's overpowered someone. He is obsessed with being popular, but I'd say it's NOT working. For some reason he thinks it is or it will.

I hate to see Gavin humiliate people. It feels sickening and I am not even involved. Still I feel like a jerk judging Gavin; I heard how harsh it is for him at home. His mom is only about as old as my sister; that can't be easy. I hear he was regularly kicked around as a kid and then laughed at when he cried. Some people have it rough. I don't know a tenth of it, I'm sure. It's easy to see how someone could have some really bad things to think about.

November: I met a new guy at school this year, Kyle, and he is super friendly and just himself. He has a way of including people who aren't connected. He's interested and cares about all kinds of people and best of all he's funny. He's confident and no one even tries to intimidate him; he just connects with everybody. I am hoping Kyle will begin to build a relationship with Gavin and maybe burst Gavin's bravado bubble. Kyle says he will get the chance to connect with Gavin, so time will tell.

March: BTW Kyle has gotten to know Gavin and I have noticed a change already. Gavin's less intimidating now. It turns out he can be funny sometimes and it's nice that it's not always at someone's expense. I was really surprised to see Gavin change even a little. Proof that anyone can change and show signs of social responsibility.

Okay, back to it … The most intense story relating to what we are learning is about Sarah and Ruby, two ex-friends, and their digital responsibility. I heard they used to be best friends before Sarah got a boyfriend. Ruby had had a secret crush on the same guy. Sarah had no idea! Their friendship ended when Ruby got mean to Sarah, and kept it up even after Sarah wasn't going out with him anymore.

Ruby was jealous and out to get Sarah; you could just feel it. It was clear Ruby controlled the girls in her clique; they were attractive, really popular and purposely excluded Sarah. Just mean! Ruby also spread cruel online rumors about Sarah. Clearly not digital responsibility!

April: It was after spring break that I really saw Sarah change. She used to look upbeat, but she often looks down and kind of hurt. I see changes in Ruby, too. She looks bad. Her eyes have dark circles underneath and she's tired. A friend told me Ruby also has some kind of turmoil at home; I am not really sure what. We can't always see what stuff is going on in someone's life.

At least Sarah has one friend, her cousin, Alice. I'm in English class with Alice and she tells me Ruby relentlessly sends Sarah harsh messages and is constantly harassing Sarah. It's likely Sarah doesn't feel safe anywhere. The more we learn about digital citizenship, Alice and I know this can't go on. Every time Sarah's away I wonder if it's because she's anxious and too afraid to come to school. This whole mess between Ruby and Sarah is like a train wreck in slow motion.

May: I have sensed that Ruby's messages and threats are too much for Sarah; I even saw her crying. She left campus, smoked her tires and drove off recklessly after lunch yesterday. How is it I can see all of this but I don't really know what to do? Fortunately, Alice used her good common sense and sprang into action.

She went to Sarah's that afternoon for another one of their long talks. Sarah admitted to being "done in." Alice said one of her friends got help last year when a counselor helped him to see clearly and understand life a little better. Alice knew Sarah's parents were really loving, and convinced Sarah to let her tell them about what had been going on.

Things happened super-fast after that. Ruby was called to the principal's office. Some students saw the principal, Ruby's parents, a counselor, a teacher and another adult going into the meeting. Sounds like it maybe was a Preventing Violence meeting like is written about on our school's planner app.

Someone heard Ruby shouting in the office as she was desperately defending herself. "So I said some things. It's no big deal. I was just fooling around. I wasn't threatening. I was playing around!" Then there was a definite change in her voice. Apparently she was faced with the evidence---lots of evidence of cyberbullying. I hear she broke down and lost it and then begged for an answer … "What can I do now?"

One thing's for sure, Ruby was forced to realize bullying was not the way out of her jealousy. Maybe the evidence kind of woke her up. She was probably only thinking of herself and not how it felt to be at the other end, or how serious harassment is.

Rumor has it the law was involved because an officer gave a school presentation recently. He had hacked some student online accounts pretending to be a teen girl and actually got dates with some of the guys. Sure shows how we really may not know who we are talking to. I am thinking to myself: "Big lesson! Be careful who you make a date with online!" The officer ended by saying, "Anybody engaged in online harassment, no matter how smart you are or how smart you think you are … I can find you." And guess what I discovered online? Bullying is a form of harassment in the US, UK, and Canada. Look it up for yourself:

Canada, "Criminal Harassment"
www.laws-lois.justice.gc.ca/eng/acts/C-46/section-264.html
United Kingdom, "Protection from Harassment"
www.legislation.gov.uk/ukpga/1997/40/contents

United States, "Harassment Law and Legal Definition"
www.definitions.uslegal.com/h/harassment

June: As I see it, Ruby was really a lost thinker with a second chance, just like Gavin. After suspension, Ruby sees the counselor weekly. I hear there will be a combined counseling session with Ruby and Sarah. Sarah is also lined up with another counselor. She tells Alice he explains the choice she has, to not take things others say so personally. The choice stops her from feeling terribly unhappy. Alice says there's a logic to what Sarah's learning. It's ordinary and understandable and she is encouraged to be pointed back to her own inner wisdom.

Counselor and Teacher's Perspectives

I interviewed our counselor and English teacher for this blog post. They are part of a team to wrap-around any student with a problem. They also help with the school-wide focus on social and digital responsibility. Here's what they want to add:

When we start up again in the fall we want to support students in moving forward. We are keeping these notes of things to share with students next year; we can all be part of one solution. There will be more to add as insights come to us:

1. We are beginning to understand *both* sides of bullying, which is a form of harassment. We see that accessing inner wisdom is key to solving problems and building relationships.
2. For anyone who is the aggressor in the situation, remember: "The misled thoughts of humanity, alienated from their inner wisdom, cause all violence, cruelty …" (Mis. 84) Instead of acting on misleading thoughts, connect to your inner wisdom that rightly leads to your happiness and success.
3. For anyone who is the victim in the situation, remember: "Cut off from innate wisdom, a lost thinker experiences isolation, fear and confusion." (Mis. 83) Connect to innate wisdom and experience happiness.
4. Research shows that generally, in the past decade, student harassment has been reduced and bullying is on the decline. See these links:

www.news.ubc.ca/2016/02/23
https://study.com/blog/is-school-bullying-really-declining-a-recent-study-shows-it-is.html
www.adjacentgovernment.co.uk/education-schools-teaching-news/study-reveals-bullying-decline/11629

5. We think students these days are more aware than kids were in the past. In our school we are all concerned for people being oppressed. We can be socially and digitally responsible.
6. We also know that when we're in touch with our natural inner wisdom, our **Guide Inside**, we extend compassion to a person. We can throw a life-saving line to someone in trouble on either side of the situation. With some support, each one of us can show resilience and begin to navigate life successfully. It is good to know that we can make a big difference. Everyone is part of the culture.
7. **The Article 1 Universal Declaration of Human Rights** applies globally, way beyond our school, but relates to every one of us:

> "All human beings are born free and equal in dignity and rights. They are endowed with reason and conscience and should act towards one another

in a spirit of brotherhood [and sisterhood.]" www.un.org/en/universal-declaration-human-rights.

∞

June (continued): I'd like to think when someone owns up to what they have done by taking responsibility and trying to set it right, they can do a 180 and use their personal power in a much more positive way. When we come back to school next fall I will be really curious what happens with Sarah and Ruby. What have we all learned about social media and our own responsibility?

Being on assignment for my class was an amazing journey. We all collectively hold the power by looking out for social and digital responsibility. Let's put ourselves into it; every one of us is part of the culture and owns a part of it. Even though we may not directly be part of the problem, we are all affected to varying degrees. We can directly be part of one solution.

Seems to me, it's an inside job. There is hope!

➢ **Let's talk about the big picture.**
- In any situation, innate wisdom, our guide inside, is always a choice for solving problems and building relationships. What connections did you make with the blog posts?
- What does the following true incident have in common with Sarah and Ruby's conflict? "Tech High School is a large and complex building with many wings and corridors. Two junior boys of different ethnicities crashed into each other at a hallway blind intersection. Instantly they were cursing in the worst possible way, calling each other's mothers terrible names, and taking swings. Students and teachers surrounded them. Both landed in the office and were suspended. At times the incident continued to flare up in the parking lot. Their school social worker created a young men's Three Principles support group to remediate the problem. She absolutely loved working with these guys."
- Talk about the value of the following: "Life is like any other contact sport. You may encounter hardships of one sort or another. Wise people find happiness not in the absence of such hardships, but in their ability to understand them when they occur."

(Mis. 124)

Teen Reflection: How does it resonate with you?

"I learned you will always come across suffering individuals. It is important not to overlook this. Remember they are just like you, only living in a world created by their own painful thoughts. For example, if someone is bullying you or your friend, tell a parent or a teacher. Protect yourself or your friend, and the person who is bullying. When we relate from a place of caring and understanding instead of anger and retaliation, we give others the opportunity to let go of the negative thought patterns creating their unpleasant lives. This naturally creates a more easy-going world for everyone."

"With wisdom people see beyond the filters and biases of race and culture, to realize the beauty in everyone." (Mis. 136)

MGI Chapter Resource Center

Use the resources, activities and projects provided to enhance your learning.
- **Activities**: These are for credit, grades and creativity. Use the criteria for success!
- **Just for Fun**: Enjoy a good feeling.
- **Vital Vocabulary**: Enhance communication.
- **Experiment**: Try this during the week.
- **Appendix D**: "Reminders" deepen understanding.
- **Resources Tab**: myguideinside.com includes Video On Demand to bring this chapter to life, Video Clips that enhance, and Digital Media Options for each activity. Password: mgi

Activities

❖ **Reflect and Write a Journal Entry**
- Write a reflection or respond to one of these ideas; include Vital Vocabulary words.

"Love recognizes no barriers. It jumps hurdles, leaps fences, penetrates walls to arrive at its destination full of hope." (Maya Angelou)

"Life is like any other contact sport. You may encounter hardships of one sort or another. Wise people find happiness not in the absence of such hardships, but in their ability to understand them when they occur." (Mis. 124)

Success Criteria: use "I," share thoughts, feelings; show insight, connections.

❖ **Respond to a Video Clip**
- Respond in your journal.

See Resources tab.

Success Criteria: use "I," express your ideas clearly; show insight, connections.

❖ **Create a Public Service Announcement (PSA)**
- With a small group, choose one of the main topics from the previous chapter themes or have your own unique idea approved to create a one minute PSA video. You could also select an alternate format—diagram, instruction manual, magazine article, news broadcast, slide show, skit, song or talk show interview. Present to your group and/or post on the class blog.

Chapter 1: Discover *My Guide Inside* and Understand Separate Realities
Chapter 2: The Lure of Being Secure and Masks of Insecurity
Chapter 3: Being Flawsome and Fun: Discovering our True Identity
Chapter 4: Finding Peace by Getting Past Trouble
Chapter 5: Understanding the Lost Thinker

Success Criteria: create an original text, use accurate information and with collaborative effort make an interesting presentation.

- ❖ **Create a Blog**
  - Write three blog posts about "Building Healthy Relationships." Use your own unique viewpoint and opinions. Example themes: Navigate Life with Resilience; Get Connected—Build Sound Relationships!

  Success Criteria: use original ideas which are clearly expressed, show understanding and include enhancements with accurate citations.

- ❖ **Create a Poster**
  - Create your own poster slogan based on what you are learning. Or use: No guarantee for life to be problem free.

  Success Criteria: informative and neat, effective use of space, colorful and accurate.

Just for Fun

- ✓ **Your Turn to Give Advice** … Advise someone two years younger about "using the force," inner wisdom, to solve problems and/or build relationships. Add this to your journal.

- ✓ **Candle and Cup Demonstration** … Either replicate or visualize this metaphor. In this activity assume every baby is born with a spark of light inside. It is your true self, wisdom, what we call your **Guide Inside**. Try this experiment. Place a candle on a desk and light it (or use a tiny flash light) and turn out the lights in the room. Soon your eyes adjust and the small light will illuminate the room sufficiently for to you find your way. Hold a ceramic mug about ten inches (25 cm) over the light to represent your own thinking. Slowly move the cup closer and closer to the light source. As your "busy thinking" gets close and blocks or covers up the light it becomes harder and harder to find your way. In ordinary life the more we overthink, the less we see. Lift the cup, let your thinking clear for your new insights to become known.

  (Thanks to Braden Hughs, a School Social Worker in the U.S., for sharing this activity with us!)

- ✓ **Comic Relief** … Find video clips of people naturally bursting into laughter. What happens to you? There are so many examples of laughing babies online; they get us going every time. Have you noticed how our own thinking shifts effortlessly and we feel like laughing? Share your best example(s) with the group. Still true … laughter is good medicine!

Vital Vocabulary

*Some of these words are relatively simple.
Understanding them in a deeper way will enhance your communication.*

Bravado—bold show to impress or intimidate
Brotherhood—feeling of kinship
Conscience—inner voice
Dignity—quality of being worthy of respect
Friendliness—being kind and likable
Harass—behave offensively persistently over time
Harassment—aggressive intimidation such as bullying
Immunity—protection or exemption
Intimidate—frighten
Isolation—remaining alone, not connected
Misguided—showing faulty judgment or reasoning
Oppressed—maltreated
Responsibility—accountability
Security—feeling of safety
Sisterhood—feeling of kinship
Social—relating to the group
Vulnerable—in need of support

Experiment

A real smile is a sure indicator of friendliness. Can you catch yourself smiling naturally? There is no one smiling all the time, but throughout the week notice what effect a smile has as you navigate your day.

Chapter 6
Making Room for Happiness

You can get rid of negative thoughts that stop you from living in the present. You have free will to navigate life moment-to-moment. An insight can happen anytime; however, a calm state of mind naturally produces helpful insights. With inner wisdom as your guide, you will experience happiness.

Do you know the past is only a thought you choose to carry through time? The past is your own memory. You rather naturally decide what you do with it. As you begin to learn the logic of how your own experience—reality—is created, you will notice a change in yourself. Your memories begin to shift and change as you have new insights. In this way you get a deeper, richer understanding of life. And the biggest surprise of all is that you will discover you actually have healthier feelings for yourself and also for others. The really good news is, your understanding of this inside-out nature just keeps growing.

As one teen writes, "We are learning to not allow our negative thoughts to control us. We can open our heart and change to positive thoughts."

In this chapter, we use inner intelligence to gain a healthy perspective on past experiences. Focus is on the logic of how personal experience is created by our own thinking. As a result, in a calm state of mind, we discover healthy thoughts and feelings about ourselves and others, and communicate our ideas effectively.

Kailani's Story

What do you already know about "Making Room for Happiness"?

My boss is the worst. I show up after school every day, usually on time, and do my job fine, but nothing satisfies him. He constantly picks on me, tells me to do this, do that; I know perfectly well what I have to do! When I'm done with a job, he criticizes me. If I try to stand up for myself, he says I'm being immature and rants about how there are lots of other people who would love to have this job. I hate being told what to do, especially by him, and feel like quitting, but I need the money.

My teachers give me more aggravation. I'm just trying to pass my subjects so I can graduate and get out. School is not my favorite place. I have one cool friend; everybody else is annoying. I really don't see how my friend Bailey can hang out with some of the kids at this school and be involved in clubs and stuff. She is cool and the only one who even remotely "gets" me. We've known each other since kindergarten. On Wednesdays we're in the same Health and Career class and afterwards we always have lunch together. (I'm not interested in the people Bailey eats lunch with most days.)

Bailey tells me she thinks the Three Principles we are learning in class "can help everyone have an easier time in life." She should know better than to think I'd believe anything like that. I've had my fill of so-called "expert" advice!

I've had a rough time in life; I was abused when I was younger. When I finally told my mom about it that jerk was already past history. She took me to see a "special" therapist who made me go over and over what had happened. At first it was a relief to understand I was betrayed, but remembering it all just made me feel angry. I finally refused to go.

∞

Bailey's the only one I trust and the only one I told. She has never mentioned a word to anyone. It's enough that the memories of what happened are there. The last thing I want or need is my story to get out.

When I talk about the past or about my terrible boss or about how unfair a teacher has been to me, Bailey usually tries to make me laugh by being ridiculously comical! Sometimes it doesn't work but at lunch today I couldn't help myself and we both were cracking up. It really hit me that I was lucky to have such a good friend. I was surprised when I heard myself asking, "Do you still think *anyone* can have an easier time in life?"

Bailey was quiet for a minute. "Yeah, I'm starting to think it is just common sense. In the stories we're reading, it's always basically the same. The character learns that you have free will and you don't have to go with every thought that comes into your head. I get that we actually have a choice about which thoughts to go with. Makes logical sense that if we ignore the useless thoughts and mostly go with the useful ones, we'll have an easier time in life. Do you remember we heard that guy say that you flick away the useless thoughts like you would a bug on the back of your neck?"

"Ha!" I replied. "Maybe that's true for you and the people we've been reading about, but not me. When people are mean or unfair to me I feel so angry; I can't stop thinking about it. I definitely don't have a choice. And I would never choose to still be haunted by my past, but I am."

It had been a nice distraction to laugh with my friend, but reality came crashing back. I felt a knot in my stomach as I remembered how crummy my life was.

"If it wasn't for you, Bailey, I wouldn't have a friend in the world. Life is hard for me. You know what I've been through, and now isn't much better. I just can't seem to catch a break." My voice broke. Despair and anger swept over me.

Bailey reached out and hugged me. Her calmness was comforting; "I think it's just about finding a good feeling—that's really all it is. Like when we were laughing like crazy before, didn't you feel good?"

"Yeah, for a few minutes." I admitted. "Like I said, if not for you …"

"But it's not me that made you feel good. Sometimes you don't even crack a smile when I make one of my brilliant jokes." I had to admit that was true and it really had nothing to do with how great the joke was.

"So if you can be happy for a few minutes, it proves you've got it in you!"

This was all new to me, and the exact opposite of everything I'd heard about people being "scarred" by things in their past.

I liked the way Bailey saw what we were learning. I still wondered if it was really true for me given what I'd experienced. After work, which surprisingly was not as bad as usual, I sat in the shade of my favorite big, old tree and read the new handout from our class.

As I sat reading the handout in the shade of that big old tree, something happened that I can't explain. It just felt like what I was reading was true, even for me: "The past no longer exists." I felt hope and overwhelming relief. For the first time, I could see I didn't have to let the thoughts about my past control my life—I saw that I am safe now and can experience a state of well-being. The feeling was so new to me. Bailey was right; insights can totally turn things around.

It's been six months since our class ended, and my life is so much better. I'm not distracted by angry thoughts about every little thing that happens. I even stopped thinking about getting back at the guy who hurt me. I don't want to go there anymore. I'm remembering other parts of my past like nice times with my mom and my cousins. When a bad memory comes up I know it's just a passing thought. I don't get into feeling so angry. I realize I'm okay.

I even appreciate my teachers and boss a bit. They seem so much nicer. My mom sees how much better I am; sometimes she asks me what I learned. We talk a little and I think it's helping her feel better. Some days I even wonder if I might be able to help younger kids. Time will tell.

Mental Health: Your State of Well-being

Everyone has experienced hard times to some degree. Everyone has "stuff" that no one else sees. Author Sydney Banks agrees that many students have difficult things happen in their lives and offers us a way to our own state of well-being.

How will you use these ideas in your own life?

∞

"If you're going through school and you're studying,
you can't possibly study well
if your mind is full of a lot of negative thoughts,
negative feelings, and negative memories.
The more you can live in the now,
the better chance you have of being a good student." (Att. 3:33)

∞

"The second your mind calms down …
you get what you call an insight.
A sight from within, deep past your personal mind
and all of a sudden your world changes
and the past starts to dissipate.
It starts to become no longer of any value.
It has no longer any control over you." (One 3:13)

∞

"The past no longer exists. …
Memory is a thought carried through time
and it creates an illusion that it is still a reality,
but in fact, it is not a reality.
This is why going back into the past …
to try and find mental health, is really a fallacy. It really is." (Att. 4:05)

➢ **Think, pair, share**
- The logic of letting go of the past to make room for happiness is always the same. How is the logic in this story like something you know?
- Talk about Kailani's pivotal moments. What may have caused Kailani's boss and teachers' dispositions to change?

Five Years Later...
Lilianna's Story

©Jane Tucker, 1999, Middletown, MD (adapted 2016)

How do Kailani and Lilianna's stories connect?

"Lilianna, can you tell us about a special event during your holidays?"

The ten-year old squirmed in her seat, eyes down, and said nothing, hoping her teacher would give up and move on to the boy next to her.

"Please share with us, Lilianna." Everyone waited. Close to tears, Lilianna shook her head. Then in desperation she looked up and pointed to her neck, mouthing the words, "Can't talk—sore throat."

Mr. Perez looked like he didn't believe her. "Alright Lilianna, you can pass. Marcus, how about you?" One by one, different kids talked about visiting relatives far away, helping serve a holiday dinner, and even going to a museum dinosaur exhibit. The teacher wrote lots of suggestions on the smartboard and asked the students to write a story about their most memorable holiday event.

Lilianna felt her hands shaking. She always had trouble writing; a whole story was just too much! She was good in class—never made trouble. You'd think Mr. Perez would leave her alone. He was always calling on her. They'd probably have to read their stories out loud and Lilianna just knew she would get picked first.

She stared at the blank computer screen wondering why her life had to be so different from other kids'. She thought of her last session with Ms. B. who was supposed to be helping her. Ms. B said what happened wasn't her fault. So why did she have to keep talking about it? As Lilianna's memories returned, she felt more alone and miserable than ever.

Lilianna heard Mr. Perez say, "Okay class, it's lunchtime soon. Save your stories."

She looked at the empty screen in front of her. She hated school. She was having so much trouble they arranged for her to go to a tutor twice a week. It was just one more thing that made her feel different.

∞

She barely spoke to the tutor, a fourth year college student in the Education Assistant program. Lilianna made it obvious she did not want to be there and didn't make eye contact. Her tutor, Kailani, didn't seem to mind. She made cards and asked Lilianna to put the words together into sentences. Then Kailani read the sentences aloud, as if they were the most interesting ideas in the world. Hearing her, Lilianna almost felt good at writing. The tutor invented word games, and gave Lilianna a special high five when she won a round.

Gradually, Lilianna came to look forward to time with Kailani because she could just be herself. It was a relief not to feel pressured to say or do anything. The games were kind of fun, especially if she won.

One afternoon, Kailani read Lilianna a story: "A girl played under a big tree. The golden sun was shining. There were fluffy clouds and a rainbow in the sky. She found a furry puppy, and she taught him tricks. He jumped through a hoop and danced around. One day a circus came to town …" The story went on for three pages. Lilianna couldn't believe they were her ideas.

"I told you that you could write!" Kailani beamed. "That story is filled with your ideas. Do you want to paint a picture to go with it?"

Kailani produced a box of paints and

brushes and Lilianna created a scene with the golden sun, a big tree and a furry puppy. She painted a girl with curly hair and overalls in the middle of the picture, but she couldn't get the face right. Every time she tried to do the smile, it turned into a frown. The eyes were supposed to be happy, but they looked mad. The more she worked on it, the messier it got.

Kailani noticed her frustration. "Having trouble?"

"She just keeps staying mad," the girl whispered.

"What's she thinking about?"

"Mad thoughts." Lilianna's voice was tense.

"Doesn't she know she can get a different idea?"

Lilianna looked puzzled and gave a shrug.

"Lilianna, I learned something in school that still really helps me. We don't have to keep thinking mad or sad thoughts. Just because a thought pops into your head doesn't mean you have to keep it alive. You can choose to let it just pass by."

Lilianna shook her head. "The girl in the picture can't do that."

"Well, you're the artist! You can help her notice a fresh thought. Every one of us has a **Guide Inside**; it's our common sense or inner wisdom and it leads us to our happiness. Maybe she doesn't know that. It's kind of like the sun you painted. Did you ever look up at the sky and see clouds covering up the sun?"

Lilianna nodded.

"Even though the clouds block it temporarily, the sun is still there, right?"

"Yeah…"

"When we're feeling angry (or sad, or fearful), it's just because we're thinking those kinds of thoughts. When we let those thoughts pass by like clouds, our natural happiness, like the sun, shines through and we feel good again."

Lilianna stiffened and looked down at the picture again. "This girl doesn't have happiness inside. Bad things happened to her. She's all bad and angry inside." Lilianna blinked back her tears and compassion rose up in Kailani.

She said softly, "Lilianna, I understand. I used to feel the same way until I found out that nothing—nothing—can damage who I really am, inside.

Whatever happened to you in the past, it's not who you are now. Just like whatever happened to me in the past and all the thinking I did about it is not who I am now. I know I am healthy now, and that feeling just gets deeper and deeper."

Lilianna, for the first time, lifted her head and looked straight into Kailani's eyes, as if searching for proof of something. Finally, she asked, "Honest?"

"Honest." Kailani replied.

Slowly, a smile spread across Lilianna's face. She picked up the brush and easily painted a smile for the little girl in the picture! "No more mad eyes!"

After sharing a high-five, Kailani said, "The picture you painted is beautiful, and you deserve to enjoy a life that's beautiful, too. Just remember that feelings come from thoughts. Your **Guide Inside** is always there to help you—it *is* you—and it will lead you to the good thoughts! We both love to paint and this quote helps me …"

"Your thoughts are like the artist's brush. They create a *personal* picture of the reality you live in." (Mis. 56)

This was the beginning of a conversation that continued throughout the tutoring that spring. Lilianna kept learning about her true self, wisdom, her **Guide Inside**. It could always be trusted to lead her in the right direction. She discovered that if a memory she didn't like came to mind and she didn't grab onto it, it would go away, like a cloud passing across the sun in the sky. Over time, the bad memories came less frequently. By letting go of them, she made room for happiness in her life.

∞

Kailani kept Mr. Perez and Lilianna's mother up-to-date about Lilianna's progress. Lilianna also talked to her mom about her time with Kailani. They decided she really didn't need any more sessions with Ms. B.

Over time, Lilianna came to truly enjoy learning, became optimistic and interested in everything around her. She forgot to be shy and felt secure when she had something to share.

At Kailani's exit interview, Mr. Perez remarked on the changes he saw in Lilianna. "How in the world did you get that stubborn little snail to come out of her shell?"

"Oh, I never saw any stubborn little snail," Kailani laughed. "Just an innocent girl who was lost in a bunch of negative thoughts. To tell you the truth, she reminded me of myself when I was younger, and my heart went out to her. I'm grateful I was lucky enough to learn the Three Principles when I did. It woke me up to my own inner wisdom, the **Guide Inside** everyone has that can never be damaged and is always available. If I hadn't learned that, I wouldn't have had a clue how to help Lilianna find her happiness."

∞

That summer, as Kailani was walking to a friend's house, she ran into Lilianna returning from the library.

"Hi Kiddo! How's your summer going?"

Lilianna smiled and said, "Good, thanks!"

She held up her cloth book bag, and Kailani peeked inside.

"Oh, I know this one from my high school days!" Kailani exclaimed, pulling a slim volume out of the bag as if it were a long-lost friend. "'Dear Liza' is one of my favorites." On the cover was a soft sketch of a young girl from long ago, sitting peacefully and reading from an open book. Kailani leafed through the familiar pages, and was especially touched to see a passage from one of the letters to Liza from her mother: "Again I tell you, look very closely, my daughter, at love and compassion for they are the two magical feelings that will help guide you through life. Such feelings are more powerful than any king's army." (Dear 71)

Lilianna watched Kailani silently reading and, after a moment, placing the book gently back in the bag. Kailani paused briefly and said, "My most favorite quote from another book by this author is: *Among the greatest gifts given to us are the powers of free thought and free will, ... enabling us to see life as we wish.*" (Mis. 50)

"We are both so lucky we learned to let go of our old painful memories. We 'see life as we wish' now." They shared a hug and continued on their separate ways.

> **Let's talk about the big picture.**
- Consider the following: How are Kailani and Lilianna similar? What caused Lilianna to effortlessly paint a smile? Is it true in their stories that knowledge is a baton that keeps getting passed on?
- Talk about the logic of this quote: "Let your negative thoughts go. They are nothing more than passing thoughts. You are then on your way to finding the peace of mind you seek, having healthier feelings for yourself and for others. This is simple logic." (Mis. 108)

Teen Reflection: How does it resonate with you?

"The main idea is to keep a clear mind and be positive. We are learning to not allow our negative thoughts to control us. We can open our heart and change to positive thoughts. We can understand others have problems. As our hearts open we are able to forgive. Do not allow your negative thoughts to control you. Search yourself for the 'aloha' feeling."

What do you see in these illusions?

"Memory is a thought carried through time and it creates an illusion." (Att. 4:05)

MGI Chapter Resource Center

Use the resources, activities and projects provided to enhance your learning.
- **Activities**: These are for credit, grades and creativity. Use the criteria for success!
- **Just for Fun**: Enjoy a good feeling.
- **Vital Vocabulary**: Enhance communication.
- **Experiment**: Try this during the week.
- **Appendix D**: "Reminders" deepen understanding.
- **Resources Tab**: myguideinside.com includes Video On Demand to bring this chapter to life, Video Clips that enhance, and Digital Media Options for each activity. Password: mgi

Activities

❖ **Reflect and Write a Journal Entry**
- Write a reflection or respond to one of these ideas; include Vital Vocabulary words.

"Let your negative thoughts go. They are nothing more than passing thoughts. You are then on your way to finding the peace of mind you seek, having healthier feelings for yourself and others. This is simple logic." (Mis. 108)

"What lies behind you and what lies in front of you, pales in comparison to what lies inside of you." (Waldo Emerson)

Success Criteria: use "I," share thoughts, feelings; show insight, connections.

❖ **Respond to a Video Clip**
- Respond in your journal.

See Resources tab.

Success Criteria: use "I," express your ideas clearly; show insight, connections.

❖ **Persuasive Writing**
- Create your own topic to persuade the reader based on what you are learning. Or: The past is only an illusion; persuade the reader to consider letting go of the past.

Success Criteria: state point of view boldly, include convincing reasons, organize logically, use correct conventions and call for "action."

❖ **Fast Forward Profiling**
- Lilianna graduates high school in about five years. Write her first "LinkedIn" profile Include: memorable headline, education, background summary, list of skills, job and volunteer experience, groups joined and goals. Or, if you are 14 or older, check with your teacher or parent to get support to create your own first "LinkedIn" profile for real.

Success Criteria: engaging headline, concise summary, interests reveal personality, experience (paid and unpaid) and thoughtful goals.

- ❖ **Volunteering**
  - Create a real volunteer opportunity for yourself. Perhaps you can learn something new while also sharing what you know. Responsibility can, ironically, equal freedom. As a bonus, you may "find" yourself when you "lose" yourself in something worthwhile. Whether you are petting kittens or involved with humanitarian efforts, volunteering is valuable preparation for adulthood.

  Success Criteria: accurate work, be responsible, show initiative, good attitude and consistent attendance.

- ❖ **Song Lyrics Review**
  - Write your interpretation of the song lyrics video, *I Won't give Up* by Jason Mraz. Give attention to "deeper meanings" and the BIG picture. Focus on some or all of these key words: love, humanity, compassion, optimism, positivity, and resilience.

  Success Criteria: convey song's meaning, show thought and reflection, give example of poetic device, use clear and accurate conventions.

Just for Fun

- ✓ **Enjoy video clip** …
  Illusions

Vital Vocabulary

Some of these words are relatively simple.
Understanding them in a deeper way will enhance your communication.

Aloha—Hawaiian word meaning love, understanding, peace and compassion
Antidote—something that counteracts unpleasant feeling
Betrayed— trust has been violated
Dissipate—disappear
Honesty—quality of being trustworthy
Ignore—refuse to take notice
Memory—recollection
Resilience—capacity to navigate life
Rewarded—receiving what one deserves
Ruminate—dwell on

Experiment

Throughout the week, be aware of what's on your mind. If you are ruminating about the past; let it go! Feel the freedom. Let your mind clear; notice how that naturally makes room for happiness.

Chapter 7
Facing the Future in a State of Well-being

You can look to the future with hope. It is true. Inner wisdom is always available and you will see that worry, anxiety and overwhelm are needless thoughts that distract you from success. There's no common sense in using your thoughts against yourself! Happiness, well-being and a feeling of security go hand in hand. Your own good attitude is an outcome of understanding the logic of the Three Principles.

As one teen advises, "It's like a sugar pill, if you think that you'll feel insecure, then you will. Get past that, then you're as good as golden, 'cause beyond that it's just physical ability to get work done. Just think about everyone else who's gone through this same obstacle and who's succeeded, they're not much different from who you are."

In this chapter, we find hope, happiness and well-being. Focus is on discovering that learning the Three Principles Equation has the natural outcome of a good attitude. Worry, anxiety and overwhelm become needless and distracting.

Bryon's Story

Byron is completing an assignment for his senior Grad Transitions requirements. His journal is a response to a podcast called "Attitude!"
Here are sample excerpts from the podcast.

"Now being students, if you use those Three Principles and you create in your own head the feeling of insecurity then you will go through life and go through school as an insecure person. On the other hand, if you use those three gifts to create security, then this is how you will go through life, as a secure person because it truly is a world created from our own thoughts." (Att. 1:20)

"A lot of people...worried all the way through life... till they realized how the principles worked. These principles turn their thought system into logic and logic is: whatever you think, that's what you are. If you think you're insecure, you're going to be an insecure person. If you think you're a loving person, you'll be a loving person." (Att. 10:06)

"You work from the same Three Principles as anybody else. You have a free will like anybody else. And deep inside you, lies this innate mental health, this innate wisdom. ... And if you can clear away all those negative thoughts, and start feeling good about yourself, this wisdom will come out." (Att. 11:15)

"One of the very main things in life for a student is attitude. If your attitude towards your studies is good, then you'll have a good life. But if your attitude is wrong ... it fills the mind with doubt. ... And truly, truly the only difference between a good attitude and a bad one, again, is thought." (Att. 15:14)

What do you know about the chapter title: Facing the Future in a State of Well-being? As you read, consider the questions after each of Byron's journal entries.

Entry 1: I'm kind of embarrassed to write about this because I can see that others are struggling so much more than I am. I've always done well in school and never really had a problem with exams, but lately I've really started to worry. I know it has to do with the fact that next year Tech School or University (I was accepted by both—early admissions) will be so much harder than high school. I keep thinking that if I don't get the highest grades possible now, I'll start out with strikes against me. And even if I stay on top here, that doesn't guarantee I'll be able to keep up in those classes! I am feeling overwhelmed about the future.

Thought: *What might happen if Byron continues to worry about his academics?*

Entry 2: I think I get this "Mind + Consciousness + Thought = Reality" (Enl.G.R. 42) equation. But, I am puzzled. I've never been one of those kids who failed and thought, "I can't learn." I see the logic of how a thought like "I can't learn" or "I'm not as good as them" is a seed that grows and takes over.

But I'm intelligent. In fact, that is what I'm known for! That is what makes this anxiety I'm feeling so mystifying! I am so used to my parents and others saying I am the "best and brightest." It scares me to think I might not measure up in the future.

I'm not the best at sports, so I quit basketball and soccer. I didn't like playing because there was no way I would ever be one of the top players. I really don't like that feeling. I'm realizing I've had a bad attitude towards fun. Why do I have to be the best all the time? When I was a kid sports were fun.
Thought: *How can Bryon enjoy life more rather than holding himself back?*

Entry 3: I've never, ever thought of myself as insecure. I mean, really? Why would I? But worry seems kind of like insecurity. Maybe there is something to learn here. I feel some relief as I write this. Wow! If it's really just my own worried thoughts causing the feelings I've been having, I could be free to let those thoughts go. Can it be this simple? I can't believe I am smiling right now. … Thank you, Three Principles! Knowing about innate wisdom and the Three Principles really can change how you feel. I didn't get that before. It's different from analyzing a problem, but it seems to be the answer.
Thought: *What are the benefits of Byron learning about free will?*

Entry 4: I feel so much more relaxed. I really was using my own thoughts against myself without realizing it. Now I remember "worry" is only insecure thought and I can just flick it away. I was fooling myself; but my true self, my innate wisdom, knows better. I can't really describe it, but instead of being overwhelmed I have well-being inside of me. My mind is calmer and I enjoy life more. It's like my friend said, with a calm mind, you will solve a problem faster. With a calm mind, there is more room to think.

I surprised myself yesterday. I was passing the park and saw kids I know shooting hoops. I walked over and asked to join them. For the first time probably since I was a little kid, I enjoyed playing basketball with no agenda or worry about how I played, no thinking I had to be the best. I missed an easy shot and I actually laughed about it instead of feeling embarrassed or humiliated.
Thought: *Have you ever gotten lost in an activity and simply enjoyed yourself?*

Entry 5: Now that I'm starting to see how thought works, I decided to try an experiment. My kid brother Anton can be a real pest. I love him, but he intentionally bugs me on a regular basis. I thought I'd see if that could change. I logically know feelings come from thoughts, so if I keep my thoughts "chill" then my feelings should follow suit and I would not get bugged by him.

Well, it worked! When Anton pulled his usual tricks, poking me, running away or taunting me, I didn't play the game. In the past he always knew exactly what reaction he'd get from me. I'd get fed up, be aggressive and he'd get upset and I'd get in trouble.

When I didn't react to him—I just ignored the thoughts in my head—I stayed calm and positive. Believe it or not, he stopped being annoying and we actually have been getting along. Interesting how the 'rents are easing up on us … like they're relieved to have some peace in the house.
Thought: *What happens when you don't react or play "the game" with another in your life?*

Entry 6: I wanted to be the best, and since school work came pretty easy for me, that's where I zeroed in. Since learning the principles my old stressful feeling is gone. I didn't decide to change; it just happened. It's weird I never noticed the worry until I realized I was more relaxed. I can see thoughts about "being the best" took away any calm feeling. Now I choose not to go with worrisome thoughts. I guess I started listening to my innate wisdom, my **Guide Inside**.

I still study a lot, but it's more interesting. I'm not distracted by my ambition to be the best at all costs. I'm doing just as well as I was before and am actually doing some social things. I've even been playing more basketball, just for fun.

My twin sister, my best friend, is very athletic and spends a lot time in sports. She has noticed the change in me. She says I've gained perspective and have gotten over myself. She used to feel a lot of pressure to help me keep up my intellectual image. I had no idea she worried about me! She said, "You seem to have a happiness that wasn't there before." I have started sharing what I've learned with her. I am so grateful for the logic of the principles. I feel like the future has really opened up for me.

➢ **Let's talk about the big picture.**
- How are Byron's journal entries like your experience?

Consider this: "One of the very main things in life for a student is attitude. If your attitude towards your studies is good, then you'll have a good life. But if your attitude is wrong … it fills the mind with doubt. … And truly, truly the only difference between a good attitude and a bad one, again, is thought." (Att. 15:14)

Teen Reflection: How does it resonate with you?

"'Attitude' was helpful 'cause quite often in school, I'd see a couple of friends go on about how the work was almost impossible. They'd get more and more stressed and kind of flustered. The feeling of insecurity was not helping my work or thoughts. I just kept my head down and kept working and insecurity would just go on its own. It's kind of like dominoes, once you can push the first one down, they'll keep going.

When you think about being insecure, it will kind of block up everything else. It's like a sugar pill, if you think that you'll feel insecure, then you will. Get past that, then you're as good as golden, 'cause beyond that it's just physical ability to get work done. Just think about everyone else who's gone through this same obstacle and who's succeeded, they're not much different from who you are."

"If your attitude towards your studies is good, you'll have a good life." (Att. 15:14)

What do you tend to choose, moment-to-moment, for yourself?

Lifestyle A: happiness, well-being, security, good attitude and success.
Lifestyle B: anxiety, stress, insecurity, bad attitude and failure.

"Thought is the creative agent we use to direct us through life." (Mis. 47)

My Guide Inside® (Learner Book III)

MGI Chapter Resource Center

Use the resources, activities and projects provided to enhance your learning.
- **Activities**: These are for credit, grades and creativity. Use the criteria for success!
- **Just for Fun**: Enjoy a good feeling.
- **Vital Vocabulary**: Enhance communication.
- **Experiment**: Try this during the week.
- **Appendix D**: "Reminders" deepen understanding.
- **Resources Tab**: myguideinside.com includes Video On Demand to bring this chapter to life, Video Clips that enhance, and Digital Media Options for each activity. Password: mgi

Activities

❖ **Reflect and Write a Journal Entry**
- Write a reflection or respond to one of these ideas; include Vital Vocabulary words.

"One of the very main things in life for a student is attitude. If your attitude towards your studies is good, then you'll have a good life. But if your attitude is wrong … it fills the mind with doubt. … And truly, truly the only difference between a good attitude and a bad one, again, is thought." (Att. 15:14)

"Have the courage to follow your heart and intuition. They somehow already know what you truly want to become." (Steve Jobs)

Success Criteria: use "I," share thoughts, feelings; show insight, connections.

❖ **Respond to a Video Clip**
- Respond in your journal.

See Resources tab.

Success Criteria: use "I," express your ideas clearly; show insight, connections.

❖ **Sharefest**
- Divide into two groups. Group 1 discuss the personal benefits of a hopeful worldview. Group 2 explore the advantages of a learner having perspective. Form a large group to share the relevance of having hope and perspective in your lives. How can you shape your future?

Success Criteria: participate actively, be thoughtful, confident, communicate effectively.

❖ **Interview Report**
- Interview an adult you respect. Make a written report to present. Discover their view of being successful in high school and later as an adult. Ask original questions or use these samples: What important event affected your future? Who do you admire most and why? What is your best advice for me, other students?

Success Criteria: interview engages viewer with relevant information; report has clear central idea, is engaging and fluent, uses clear and correct conventions.

- ❖ **Create a Dream Theme**
  - Write about a dream you have for your future. Discuss this dream with an adult. Do you agree with this statement: "If you can dream it, you can do it." (Walt Disney)

  Success Criteria: use "I," share thoughts, feelings; show insight, connections.

Just for Fun

- ✓ **Song Lyric Review** ... Present your Song Lyrics Review as assigned in Chapter 6.
- ✓ **Learning for Fun** ... In the teen years it's super easy to learn another skill or enhance a talent by taking a new course or doing self-directed learning. Now is the time to take healthy risks and learn something new. What can you learn or learn better just for fun?

Vital Vocabulary

Some of these words are relatively simple.
Understanding them in a deeper way will enhance your communication.

Anxiety—a feeling of worry
Attitude—feeling about something
Clarity—quality of being certain; seeing clearly
Doubt—feeling uncertain
Hopeful—feel positive about the future
Insecure—feeling unsafe
Intuition—knowing from instinctive feeling
Ironic—paradoxical
Perspective—view a situation in a wise and reasonable way
Potential—possible
Secure—safe
Stress—mental strain or tension
Worry—allow one's mind to dwell on troubles

Experiment

Notice your state of mind right now. Remember a good attitude is basically a good feeling --- a state of mind you can always find. Throughout the week, notice the subtle or great benefits you experience with a good attitude. This ability to shift is naturally yours!

Chapter 8
Defining Your Individual Path

Congratulations! You are ready to review your most important lessons to be prepared for the best life possible. Remember what you already know:

Your guide inside is inner wisdom. Happiness is a state of mind, and separate realities mean we each see the world in our own unique way. You will experience more security if you let go of insecure thoughts.

Moods are simply caused by the thoughts you hold on to. Moods naturally fluctuate as your thinking shifts and flows. Stop paying attention to distressful or contaminated thinking, and you end up "in the zone" more of the time. Furthermore, the past is past. Because the past is tied to your thinking, paying attention to your insights guides you to natural wisdom and joy. Be gentle on yourself and others when the "lost thinker" temporarily seems real. Remember, when you are calm, it is easier to notice insights and drop unhelpful thinking. A new perspective will always show up. No matter what, worry is useless and a calm state of mind naturally produces a good attitude.

In this final chapter, you are invited to synthesize your learning and realize this growth occurs lifelong. This chapter focuses on remembering what you have learned as you go forward in life. You are encouraged take advantage of wonderful multi-media activities. This final session invites you to create, share and enjoy what you understand about your Guide Inside.

Facing the Future

As you complete this course you can trust that Three Principles learning deepens and continues for a lifetime. Especially remember this simple truth: "Those who have found a balance between their intelligence and their innate wisdom are the lucky ones." (Mis. 133) Let's be counted among the lucky ones! Einstein reinforces, "There will come a point in everyone's life, where only intuition can make the leap ahead, ... one must accept intuition as a fact." Know we can synchronize intelligence and innate wisdom for full benefit as we "make the leap ahead!"

Teen Reflection: How does it resonate with you?
"The most valuable aspect of this class has been to change my mood and to think positively about myself, to feel better. It changed my life because when I think about it, it all makes sense and fits together. Good thoughts produce good moods. Bad thoughts create bad moods. Our reality is created by our thought. If everyone had an understanding of Three Principles, it would be a much better place."

MGI Chapter Resource Center

Use the resources, activities and projects provided to enhance your learning.
- **Activities**: These are for credit, grades and creativity. Use the criteria for success!
- **Just for Fun**: Enjoy a good feeling.
- **Vital Vocabulary**: Enhance communication.
- **Experiment**: Try this during the week.
- **Appendix D**: "Reminders" deepen understanding.
- **Resources Tab**: myguideinside.com includes Video On Demand to bring this chapter to life, Video Clips that enhance, and Digital Media Options for each activity. Password: mgi

Activities

❖ **Assess Progress**
- Please complete the Learner Post-Assessment in Appendix B and compare to your Pre-assessment. Discover your own progress!

❖ **Reflect and Write a Journal Entry**
- Write about the most valuable aspect of this class for you. This can be an additional post-assessment of your learning.
Success Criteria: use "I," share thoughts, feelings; show insight, connections.

❖ **Create a Belonging Map**
- Listen to your common sense … sometimes you need to seek help and sometimes you can offer help. Remember what Sarah learned in Chapter 5, "My natural inner wisdom, my **Guide Inside**, helps me; sometimes it helps me know to get help." Create a *Belonging Map* with yourself in the center. Add names of people in your family, school, outside life and community who can support you. Clearly your own inner wisdom is your ultimate (24/7) source of guidance. Share your Belonging Map with an adult you know. Can the adult suggest other names you may choose to add?
Success Criteria: Be thoughtful, show links, be accurate, make it relevant.

❖ **Create a Personal Metaphor**
- The way story characters saw themselves changed over time, as they gained an understanding of their *Guide Inside*. Create a poster or presentation of your own, a Personal Metaphor, a snapshot of how you like to see yourself. Use creativity to make an image, like an owl, or another symbol of your attributes. Include descriptors to enhance your personal metaphor. For example: "Like everyone, I have wisdom inside. I am also _____, _____, and _____." Include at least three words in your poster or presentation from these many attributes:

Adventurous	Brave	Compassionate	Creative
Amiable	Calm	Compliant	Curious
Appreciative	Careful	Confident	Demonstrative
Aspiring	Caring	Conscientious	Determined
Balanced	Cheerful	Considerate	Diplomatic
Big-hearted	Companionable	Co-operative	Dreamer
Empathetic	Idealistic	Open-minded	Secure
Energetic	Imaginative	Optimistic	Selfless
Even-minded	Independent	Organized	Sensible
Fair	Inventive	Original	Sensitive
Flexible	Keen-minded	Outspoken	Sociable
Friendly	Kind	Patient	Spontaneous
Fun-loving	Level-headed	Perceptive	Tactful
Generous	Light-hearted	Persistent	Thrifty
Grateful	Likable	Practical	Trusting
Happy	Lively	Precise	Thoughtful
Hardworking	Logical	Resourceful	Understanding
Helpful	Loving	Respectful	
Hopeful	Lucid	Responsible	
Humorous	Magnanimous	Responsive	

Success Criteria: Make your poster or presentation images strong, with true qualities, use space effectively and be precise.

My Guide Inside® *(Learner Book III)*

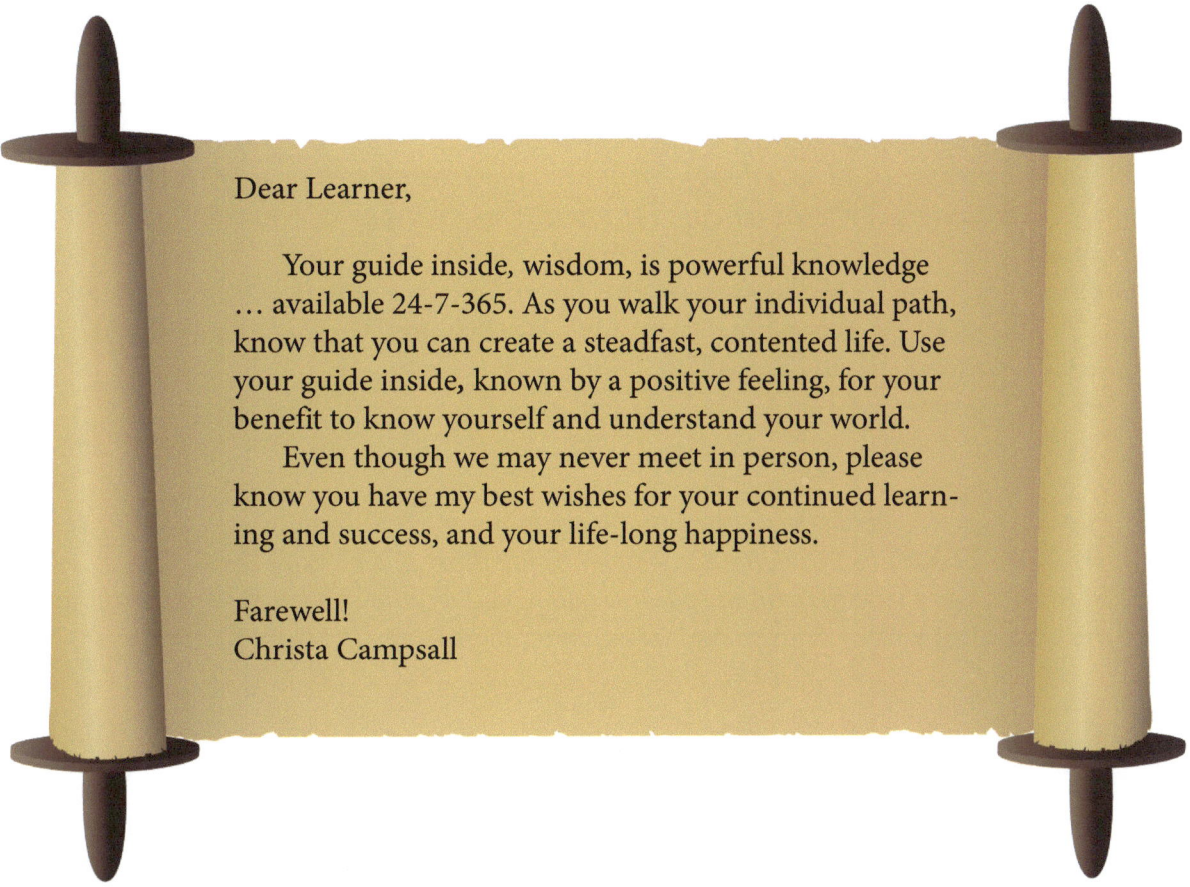

Dear Learner,

    Your guide inside, wisdom, is powerful knowledge … available 24-7-365. As you walk your individual path, know that you can create a steadfast, contented life. Use your guide inside, known by a positive feeling, for your benefit to know yourself and understand your world.
    Even though we may never meet in person, please know you have my best wishes for your continued learning and success, and your life-long happiness.

Farewell!
Christa Campsall

Teens Have the Last Word!

*"I started experimenting with [this] at home. For one week, I tried to never let my **Guide Inside** get clouded up. I just put my negative thoughts on the back burner. At the end of the week, I realized that I hadn't argued with my parents or I hadn't gotten mad at my pest of a brother. I was much happier.*

When my parents and I had a disagreement, I simply remembered separate realities and we found a fast conclusion. My inner wisdom is coming more naturally now that I know what it is, and how to use it.

Thirdly, during gym I usually get frustrated. I let my mind clear to help me get over my frustration. Therefore, I've become more confident. In conclusion, I'm glad to have learned about my natural inner wisdom and I'm thankful for the experience."

***

"I [used to] get mad about something that my parents or my sisters did … I just like run for the door, slam it as hard as I can and just kind of tramp down the block to the park or something and just sit there for a long time till my parents will actually come and get me or something. Since this class I just kind of sit there and let steam off there instead of running out the door."

***

"Many people run all their lives looking for happiness. During this course, I found that having a main objective of inner peace helped me to see my way clear. When I'm thinking negatively and being bummed out, I take time to think about inner peace and I use it as a centering point. Having this way of centering myself has shown to be helpful. It was always hard for me to relax and be peaceful inside. By recognizing inner peace, it's easier for me to relax."

***

What can you add for the last, last word?

Appendices

A: Learner Pre-Assessment *MGI (Book III)*	Page 74
B: Learner Post-Assessment *MGI (Book III)*	Page 75
C: Lesson Reminders from *MGI (Book II)*	Page 76
D: Lesson Reminders from *MGI (Book III)*	Page 77
E: Guidance for Peer Counselors and Peer Mentors	Page 80
F: Vital Vocabulary A-Z	Page 81
G: Works Cited	Page 85

My Guide Inside® (Learner Book III)

Appendix A: Learner MGI III Pre-Assessment

Class _____ ID _____ Date_____

Circle one rating for each statement about yourself. Note: your teacher may instruct you to complete this form online at myguideinside.com.

"Rarely" is 1 and "Usually" is 5

PERSONAL WELL-BEING AWARENESS					
I am happy with my life.	1	2	3	4	5
I am hopeful about my future.	1	2	3	4	5
I use common sense, inner wisdom, to guide me.	1	2	3	4	5
I remain peaceful and calm in challenging situations.	1	2	3	4	5
I recognize how my own decisions and actions affect me.	1	2	3	4	5
I am aware of and responsible for my own well-being.	1	2	3	4	5
I manage my stress.	1	2	3	4	5
COMMUNICATION, THINKING, PERSONAL AND SOCIAL RESPONSIBILITY					
I communicate effectively in classroom group discussions with other students.	1	2	3	4	5
I clearly express myself in written class assignments.	1	2	3	4	5
I use digital media communication effectively.	1	2	3	4	5
I use social media to support and help others.	1	2	3	4	5
I am a capable learner.	1	2	3	4	5
I am able to get the "big picture" as I learn new things.	1	2	3	4	5
I have determination and motivation to explore new topics.	1	2	3	4	5
I see the logical results of my own thinking and actions.	1	2	3	4	5
I catch myself "going off" emotionally, am able to calm down, and return to good behavior.	1	2	3	4	5
I make responsible decisions with consideration for others and also myself.	1	2	3	4	5
I build healthy relationships with other students.	1	2	3	4	5
I am friendly, kind and likable.	1	2	3	4	5
I listen to others with clarity, curiosity, or compassion.	1	2	3	4	5
I am trustworthy and fair.	1	2	3	4	5
I am good at solving "people problems" between my friends.	1	2	3	4	5

Please save your paper or digital Pre-Assessment to compare to a Post-Assessment at the end of this class. Your teacher may also keep a copy and visit with you. Thanks for completing the survey!

My Guide Inside® (Learner Book III)

Appendix B: Learner MGI III Post-Assessment

Class _____ I ID _____ Date_____

Circle one rating for each statement about yourself. Note: your teacher may instruct you to complete this form online at myguideinside.com.

"Rarely" is 1 and "Usually" is 5

PERSONAL WELL-BEING AWARENESS					
I am happy with my life.	1	2	3	4	5
I am hopeful about my future.	1	2	3	4	5
I use common sense, inner wisdom, to guide me.	1	2	3	4	5
I remain peaceful and calm in challenging situations.	1	2	3	4	5
I recognize how my own decisions and actions affect me.	1	2	3	4	5
I am aware of and responsible for my own well-being.	1	2	3	4	5
I manage my stress.	1	2	3	4	5
COMMUNICATION, THINKING, PERSONAL AND SOCIAL RESPONSIBILITY					
I communicate effectively in classroom group discussions with other students.	1	2	3	4	5
I clearly express myself in written class assignments.	1	2	3	4	5
I use digital media communication effectively.	1	2	3	4	5
I use social media to support and help others.	1	2	3	4	5
I am a capable learner.	1	2	3	4	5
I am able to get the "big picture" as I learn new things.	1	2	3	4	5
I have determination and motivation to explore new topics.	1	2	3	4	5
I see the logical results of my own thinking and actions.	1	2	3	4	5
I catch myself "going off" emotionally, am able to calm down, and return to good behavior.	1	2	3	4	5
I make responsible decisions with consideration for others and also myself.	1	2	3	4	5
I build healthy relationships with other students.	1	2	3	4	5
I am friendly, kind and likable.	1	2	3	4	5
I listen to others with clarity, curiosity, or compassion.	1	2	3	4	5
I am trustworthy and fair.	1	2	3	4	5
I am good at solving "people problems" between my friends.	1	2	3	4	5

On a separate page, describe the most valuable aspect of MGI in relation to knowing myself and understanding my world. Compare this Post-Assessment with the Pre-Assessment completed at the start of this class. Your teacher may also keep a copy and visit it with you. Thanks for completing the survey!

Appendix C: Lesson Reminders from My Guide Inside® (Book II)

Please take a moment to recall the most valuable Three Principles lessons you have already learned. What has served you well? Is there something you would add to the list below?

My Guide Inside
- *My Guide Inside* (natural inner wisdom) is always there 24-7-365.
- A cloudy thought passes by like clouds pass by the sun in the sky.
- Your **Guide Inside** is knowledge that grows with you.
- It brings you love and compassion and leads to happiness.

Gift of Thought
- You have this gift to use as you choose. Imagine that!
- Act on the good thoughts and you'll have nothing to lose.
- You can drop a thought like a hot potato!

Valuable Insights
- Insights help us know ourselves and understand our world.

Aloha and Wisdom
- Every child is born with a "Bowl of Light" filled with aloha and wisdom.

Green Light-Go
- RED light …STOP when angry!
  YELLOW light…What might this mean?
  GREEN light…GO ahead when at peace!

Healthy friendships
- Who and what you are inside is what counts. Knowing this you are naturally welcoming, friendly and kind.

> *"Never forget one of the most fascinating and beautiful things in this life is realizing the powerful knowledge that lies within every person."* (Dear 69)

Appendix: D Lesson Reminders from My Guide Inside® (Book III)

Chapter 1 - Discovering *My Guide Inside*
- *My Guide Inside* refers to my natural wisdom.
- The Three Principles Equation: "Mind + Consciousness + Thought = Reality" (Enl.G.R. 42)
- What we do with a thought is the variable that makes a difference.
- You are not a robot!
- We have free will to choose which thoughts get our attention.
- Mental health lies inside.
- Happiness is inside.
- We each "see a separate reality." (Mis. 6)
- Each person creates his or her own movie.
- "You're as good as anybody else." (Att. 11:12)
- Literally everybody has innate wisdom inside.

Guide Inside is innate wisdom.
Happiness is a state of mind we find … inside.

Chapter 2 - The Lure of Being Secure
- When you are in touch with your **Guide Inside**, common sense and wisdom, you know if thinking is taking you off track.
- You can actually choose to stop feeding thoughts that aren't productive and keep you feeling low.
- It was just insecure thinking in a different disguise!
- You are equipped with an internal GPS—a **Guide Inside** that will lead you in the right direction, as you dismiss the distraction of insecure thinking.
- Be grateful you are the one steering the car of your life.
- "All feelings derive, and become alive, whether negative or positive, from the power of Thought." (Mis. 25)
- "Many people make the mistake of believing that their moods create their thoughts; in reality, it is their thoughts that produce their moods." (Mis. 58)

Well-being is a secure state of mind we find … inside.

Chapter 3 - Flawsome and Fun: Our True Identity
- When your head clears, an insight is more likely to become obvious to you.
- Thinking of your own self-importance interferes with happiness.
- Who and what you are inside is what counts.
- You can make amends and get a second chance to start a healthy relationship.

- "We must look past our contaminated thoughts." (Mis. 41)
- Mental clarity reveals a positive feeling. This peace and knowing is always inside you.
- "Positive thoughts and feelings will assist you to discover the mental health and wisdom that lie within you." (Mis. 112)
- "Judging your own faults or the faults of others leads to unhappiness. … Non-judgment is a contented mind." (Mis. 118)
- There is logical cause and effect in play: negative thoughts produce negative feelings and positive thoughts create positive feelings.
- Your guide inside—wisdom—is always accessible.

There's a cause and effect relationship between thoughts and feelings.

Chapter 4 - Living in the Present: Leaving the Past in the Dust
- Thoughts "create a personal picture of the reality you live in." (Mis. 56)
- "Never, never, never put yourself down." (One 7:12)
- "There is nobody … that is any better or any worse than you." (One 7:16)
- You have a choice: holding on to old thinking keeps past hurts alive, or you can be open to an insight bringing a new perspective.
- We can feel whole and healthy.

As we become grateful, peace of mind and contentment are ours to enjoy.

Chapter 5 - Understanding the Lost Thinker
- No one can take away your dignity.
- You don't have to care what others think about you; it is only what they are thinking.
- You don't have to take everything so personally and feel so unhappy.
- No matter the details of what's going on—we are all vulnerable at times and may need help to actually SEE this and gain understanding.
- Natural inner wisdom, your **Guide Inside**, helps you … sometimes even to seek help.
- No one needs to live in the shadows.

The one solution to misguided thoughts is our innate inner wisdom.

Chapter 6 - Making Room for Happiness
- Mental health is a state of well-being.
- We all have inner wisdom, always available.
- Calm state of mind naturally produces insights which are helpful.
- Past is a memory, a thought, carried through time.
- You can have "healthier feelings for yourself and for others." (Mis. 108)

There is freedom in knowing the past is past – the present is for living.

Chapter 7 - Facing the Future in a State of Well-being
- Worry is needless. Flick it away like you would a little fly.
- "Whatever you think, that's what you are." (Att. 10:06)
- With a calm mind, you will solve a problem faster.

- With a calm mind, there is more room to think.
- "Start feeling good about yourself [and] this wisdom will come out." (Att. 12:05)
- "If your attitude towards your studies is good, then you'll have a good life." (Att. 15:14)
- Happiness, well-being, a feeling of security and a good attitude go hand in hand.

**"Use your consciousness wisely. Use your thoughts wisely.
Use your mind wisely. And you can't go wrong."** (Att. 13:42)

Chapter 8 - Defining Your Individual Path
- Happiness is inside.
- *My Guide Inside* refers to my natural wisdom.
- Natural wisdom is an "inner intelligence which everyone is born with." (Att. part 2 1:00)
- "You're as good as anybody else." (Att. 11:12)
- "Mind + Consciousness + Thought = Reality" (En.R. 42)
- We have free will to choose which thoughts receive our attention.
- Each person creates their own movie.
- We each "see a separate reality." (Mis. 6)
- An image of self-importance interferes with happiness.
- Non-judgment is contentment.
- Logical cause and effect rule: negative thoughts produce negative feelings and positive thoughts create positive feelings.
- "Never, never, never put yourself down." (One 7:12)
- "Life is like any other contact sport." (Mis. 124)
- Past is a memory, a thought, carried through time.
- A calm state of mind naturally produces insights that are helpful.
- With a calm mind, there is more room to think.
- Worry is useless: flick it away like you would a little fly.
- Mental health is a state of well-being.

"If your attitude towards your studies is good, you'll have a good life." (Att. 15:14)

Appendix E: Guidance for Peer Counselors and Peer Mentors

Note: If you want to share what you have learned about Three Principles by becoming a peer counselor or peer mentor, these suggestions may be helpful to you:

- *Health of the helper*: What ultimately qualifies you to share the principles is the extent to which you reflect and demonstrate the quality of life that other students desire (called "grounding"), and your ability to share what you understand that accounts for that quality of life. [The best way to increase your effectiveness is by looking deeper into the Principles on an ongoing basis.]
- *Look to people's innate mental health, not their problems*: There is a wisdom and logic to the Principles that exists in all living things. [Everyone already has mental health within.]
- *Insight/pure intelligence*: The realization of innate wisdom or pure intelligence comes from within the listener via insight. [This is where lasting change occurs.]
- *Deepening levels of consciousness*: We have learned to keep the message simple rather than analytical and complicated. [True understanding is a matter of the heart.]
- *A conversation between friends*: There is a great value in leveling the playing field and sharing with other students as if it were a conversation between friends.
- *Listening to truth*: We learned from Syd that the truth of the Principles can only be seen via insight. No manner of trying to figure things out ever really helped. Insight can happen at any time and in any state of mind; that said, listening with a quiet mind is more conducive to insight than an active, analytical listening process.
- *Listening to others*: We learned to listen beyond someone's story to hear their wisdom, and to point them in that direction. This will help them see that they know what to do, no matter what their history has been, or what has happened to them.
- *Stick to what you know*: It is important that we stick with what we know (what is real for us) and not try to talk beyond our grounding.
- *Sharing our story*: Syd also encouraged us to share our own personal story (how we came to understand the Principles and what we saw for ourselves).
- *Connecting the dots*: When people have insights, they change. They see and hear differently and feel different, but they may not always realize this at first. Pointing this out in the context of their results has great value. It releases a feeling of hope.
- *Stick to the Principles*: The Principles empower people by pointing them to their own wisdom, creativity and natural resilience.
- *Trust your inner wisdom/pure intelligence*: Ultimately, we all want to trust and follow our own wisdom, what we personally understand.
- *Having your heart in the right place*: Syd Banks set his sights on being of service and encouraged those who learned from him to point in that direction as well.

> *Note*: We have adapted this for Peer Counselors and Peer Mentors.
> **Sharing the Principles of Mind, Consciousness, and Thought** by Elsie Spittle and Dr. George Pransky in collaboration with Three Principle Practitioners.

Appendix F: Vital Vocabulary A-Z

Understanding these words in a deeper way enhances communication competence.

A
Acceptance—the act of accepting with approval; favorable reception
Aloha—Hawaiian word meaning love, understanding, peace, compassion
Antidote—something that counteracts unpleasant feeling
Anxiety—a feeling of worry
Attitude—feeling about something

B
Betrayed—trust has been violated
Bravado—bold show to impress or intimidate
Brotherhood—feeling of kinship

C
Caricature—comically exaggerated representation
Cause—reason
Circumstances—life events or conditions
Clarity—quality of being certain; seeing clearly
Common sense—knowing to make good choices, insight, my guide inside, wisdom
Compassion—feeling of empathy
Conscience—inner voice
Consciousness—awareness, uppercase "C" denotes the principle
Contaminated—something made impure
Content—satisfied
Contentment—happiness and satisfaction
Courage—quality of facing challenges directly

D
Delusion—false impression
Depression—state caused by lack of hope
Derive from—stem from
Dignity—quality of being worthy of respect
Disarming—allaying suspicion
Disguise—conceal, hide
Dissipate—disappear

D (cont.)
Distorted—misleading, untrue
Doubt—feeling uncertain

E
Effect—result
Element—principle, foundation for a chain of reasoning
Empathy—ability to understand feelings of others
Empowerment—becoming strong and more confident

F
Fairness—justness and sensitivity to needs of others
Fallacy—failure in reasoning
Flawsome—awesome even with flaws
Free will—ability to choose which thought to act on
Friendliness—being kind and likable

G
Grateful—thankful, appreciative of the goodness of life
Guide—wise and knowing adviser, helps to navigate life

H
Happiness—well-being and contentment, a sense that life has meaning
Harmony—agreement, understanding, co-operation
Harass—behave offensively persistently over time
Harassment—aggressive intimidation such as bullying
Honesty—quality of being trustworthy
Hopeful—to feel positive about the future
Humiliate—injure someone's dignity
Humility—unassuming view of one's abilities

I
Ignore—refuse to take notice
Immunity—protection or exemption
Initiative—self-motivation
Innate—intuitive and natural
Insecure—unsafe
Insecurity—negative feeling that has no fixed form
Insight—a helpful new idea, common sense, my guide inside, wisdom
Isolation—remaining alone, not connected
Intimidate—frighten
Intuition—knowing from instinctive feeling

I (cont.)I
Intuitive—innate and natural
Invigorate—give energy to
Ironic—paradoxical

J
Jealousy—bitterness, envy
Judgment—opinion, conclusion or evaluation

L
Light-hearted—carefree
Logic—used to anticipate results of actions
Logical—makes common sense

M
Memory—recollection
Mental health—state of well-being
Metaphor—symbol of something else
Mind—source of intelligence, uppercase "M" denotes the principle
Misguided—showing faulty judgment or reasoning
Mood—state of mind caused by my thinking in the moment
My guide inside—common sense, insight, wisdom

N
Negative—bad, not wanted
Neutral—fair and unbiased, neither positive nor negative

O
Oppressed—maltreated
Optimistic—hopeful

P
Personae—mask
Personal—belonging to a particular person
Perspective—view a situation in a wise and reasonable way
Phobia—extreme fear
Positive—good, useful
Potential—possible
Pressure—stressful urgency
Principle—truth; foundation for a chain of reasoning
Psychologically—pertaining to mental functioning

R

Reality—how life looks to the thinker
Reasoning—thinking about something in a logical way
Rehabilitation—making a positive turnaround in life
Resilience—capacity to navigate life
Responsibility—accountability
Rewarded—receiving what one deserves
Ruminate—dwell on

S

Secure—safe
Security—feeling of safety
Self-image—the idea one has of one's self
Self-determination—free will
Self-importance—an exaggerated sense of one's own importance
Self-regulate—ability to stay calmly focused
Sisterhood—feeling of kinship
Skeptical—having doubts
Social—relating to the group
Spiritual—inner
State—condition or way of being that exists at a particular time
Stress—mental strain or tension

T

Thought—creative tool, capacity to think, action of thinking, uppercase "T" denotes the principle

U

Understand—to know
Understanding—using compassion and kindness as guides; awareness
Universal—belonging to all people

V

Variable—something that may vary or change that influences an outcome
Vulnerable—in need of support

W

Well-being—state of being comfortable, healthy and happy; overall satisfaction with life
Wisdom—knowing what is true or right, common sense, insight, my guide inside
Worry—allow one's mind to dwell on troubles

X, Y, Z

Appendix G: Works Cited

Note: *My Guide Inside* uses Modern Language Association (MLA) 8 guidelines. Please see the bottom of this list to find selected abbreviated citations.

Online References

"Alain Le Sage." BrainyQuote. https://www.brainyquote.com/quotes/alain_rene_le_sage_180656. Accessed 04 Jan. 2024.

"Aristotle." Goodreads. www.goodreads.com/quotes/209683-the-actuality-of-thought-is-life. Accessed 04 Jan. 2024.

"Article 1." UN. www.un.org/en/universal-declaration-human-rights. Accessed 04 Jan. 2024.

"Chief Dan George." AZQuotes. www.azquotes.com/quote/547211. Accessed 04 Jan. 2024.

"Criminal Harassment." Canada.ca. https://laws-lois.justice.gc.ca/eng/acts/c-46/section-264.html. Accessed 09 Jan. 2024.

"Einstein's Intuition." LibQuotes. https://libquotes.com/albert-einstein/quote/lbl9y8s Accessed 04 Jan. 2024.

"Harassment Law and Legal Definition." US Legal. www.definitions.uslegal.com/h/harassment. Accessed 03 Nov. 2016.

"Is School Bullying Really Declining? - A Recent Study Shows It Is." Study.com. https://study.com/blog/is-school-bullying-really-declining-a-recent-study-shows-it-is.html Accessed 09 Jan. 2024.

"Jason Mraz – Everything Is Sound [Official Lyric Video]." YouTube. https://www.youtube.com/watch?v=wYBCiN401ds. Accessed 04 Jan. 2024.

"Jason Mraz – I won't give up [Lyrics]." YouTube. https://www.youtube.com/watch?v=O1-4u9W-bns. Accessed 04 Jan. 2024.

"Jason Mraz - Living in the Moment [Official Audio Video]." YouTube. https://www.youtube.com/watch?v=YUFs_1vKYlY. Accessed 04 Jan. 2024.

"Maya Angelou." AZQuotes. www.azquotes.com/quote/8490. Accessed 04 Jan. 2024.

"Oscar Wilde." Goodreads. www.goodreads.com/quotes/19884-be-yourself-everyone-else-is-already-taken. Accessed 04 Jan. 2024.

"Oscar Wilde." Goodreads. www.goodreads.com/quotes/282056-life-is-too-important-to-be-taken-seriously. Accessed 04 Jan. 2024.

"Pharrell Williams – Happy (Official Music Video)." YouTube. https://www.youtube.com/watch?v=ZbZSe6N_BXs. Accessed 04 Jan. 2024.

"Protection from Harassment Act 1997." Gov.UK. www.legislation.gov.uk/ukpga/1997/40/contents. Accessed 09 Jan. 2024.

"Sharing the Principles of Mind, Consciousness, and Thought by Elsie Spittle and George Pransky in collaboration with Three Principle Practitioners." 3PGC. www.3pgc.org/blog/elsie-spittle-and-george-pransky-in-collaboration-with-three-principle-practitioners. Acessed 31 Aug. 2016.

"Standing up to bullies." UBC. https://news.ubc.ca/2016/02/23/standing-up-to-bullies/. Accessed 09 Jan. 2024.

"Steve Jobs." Goodreads. www.goodreads.com/quotes/445286-have-the-courage-to-follow-your-heart-and-intuition-they. Accessed 04 Jan. 2024.

"Study reveals bullying is on the decline." AdjacentOpenAccess. www.adjacentgovernment.co.uk/education-schools-teaching-news/study-reveals-bullying-decline/11629. Accessed 30 Jan. 2017.

"Sydney Banks - A Quiet Mind, animated by CoachCafe.no." YouTube. https://youtube.com/watch?v=TQZ2w2d_aEw. Accessed 04 Jan. 2024.

"Sydney Banks – Goodwill." YouTube. https://youtu.be/eJ8A4yhPOYo. Accessed 04 Jan. 2024.

"Three Principles by Sydney Banks – Animated by CoachCafe.no." YouTube. https://youtu.be/0467yPRpbBw. Accessed 04 Jan. 2024.

"Tyra Banks' New Phrase, "Flawsome" Is One We Should All Be Using." HelloGiggles. 09 May2014. www.hellogiggles.com/tyra-banks-new-phrase-flawsome-one-using. Accessed 04 Jan. 2024.

"Waldo Emerson." BrainyQuote. www.brainyquote.com/quotes/quotes/r/ralphwaldo386697. Accessed 04 Jan. 2024.

"Walt Disney." BrainyQuote. www.brainyquote.com/quotes/quotes/w/waltdisney130027. Accessed 04 Jan. 2024.

"WHO | Mental Health: A State of Well-being." WHO | Mental Health: A State of Well-being World Health Organization. Accessed 04 Jan. 2024.

Abbreviated Citations

Quotations from multiple works by Sydney Banks are cited with the abbreviations below.

Att. *Attitude!: Using the Three Principles to Deal with Stress & Insecurity.* (2003). Edmonton: Lone Pine Publishing. [audio.]

Dear *Dear Liza.* (2004). Edmonton: Lone Pine Publishing.

Enl.G. *Enlightened Gardener, The.* (2001). Edmonton: Lone Pine Publishing.

Enl.G.R. *Enlightened Gardener Revisited, The.* (2006). Edmonton: Lone Pine Publishing.

Gre.S. *Great Spirit, The.* (2001). Edmonton: Lone Pine Publishing. [audio.]

Mis. *Missing Link, The.* (1998). Edmonton: International Human Relations Consultants.

One *One Thought Away.* (2003). Edmonton: Lone Pine Publishing. [audio]

In **MGI**, for example, (Mis. 4) refers to *The Missing Link* page 4. For an audio source, such as (Att. 4:52) refers to *Attitude!* with recording counter indicated.

Acknowledgments

Sydney Banks deeply cared about young people. He knew that if we could help you, our youth, the world would be "a far, far better place." He was an ordinary man who had an experience that profoundly changed him from the inside-out. For the rest of his life, as a speaker and author, he was dedicated to sharing the universal Three Principles he uncovered: Mind, Consciousness and Thought.

As teachers, school administrators and other helping professionals learned these principles, they consistently reported unusually positive results with youth and adults in schools, mental health clinics, businesses, jails, and community agencies. The principles **MGI** shares with you focus on individuals discovering their natural inner wisdom and innate mental health. Thi s understanding is now gaining international recognition and respect. We can all be so grateful for the opportunity to explore the principles' profound life-changing message of hope.

Heartfelt thanks go to the team of volunteer dedicated professionals who assisted me in creating **MGI**. Editor Jane Tucker co-authored the intermediate edition of *My Guide Inside*, and assisted in major ways with this teen edition by contributing Lenny's and Lilianna's stories, as well as influen cing the text and other stories with her insightful suggestions. Her boundless goodwill for sharing her understanding has enriched this curriculum immensely.

Tom Tucker artfully produced the cover and this format and Jo Aucoin created our special owl graphic. Author Elsie Spittle has kindly permitted me to include *Sharing the Principles of Mind, Consciousness and Thought,* (a document she created with Dr. George Pransky, in collaboration with other practitioners). This valuable resource is adapted, with permission, for peer counselors and mentors. As author, school teacher and principal, Barb Aust, over forty years, saw the principles bring out the best in students and teachers. She and Kathy Marshall Emerson of the National Resilience Resource Center reviewed extensively and provided important links between the principles, curriculum guidelines, and sound research regarding education, resilience, and related fields. Kathy initially strongly encouraged me to undertake this curriculum and, behind the scenes assisted me extensively in co-creating the **MGI Teacher Manual** and this **Learner Book**.

Braden Hughs, a school social worker, shared the candle metaphor with us, social worker Mavis Karn shared her letter and Paul Lock, trainer and coach, shared his poem and artwork. My husband Bob Campsall contributed insights and school stories, and encouraged me every step of the way. Our son, Michael, created the accompanying website for **MGI**. For all teens and adult reviewers who offered their suggestions and moved **MGI** along, many, many thanks!

–The Author

About the Authors

Christa Campsall (right) has a 40+ year legacy teaching the principles shared in MGI. This has been the foundation of her work as a classroom teacher, learning services teacher in special education and school-based team chair. She has a BEd and DiplSpEd from University of British Columbia, and a MA from Royal Roads University. Along with MGI curriculum development, Christa facilitates professional development for educators in the global community.

Kathy Marshall Emerson (left), National Resilience Resource Center founding director, facilitates long-term school community principle based training and systems change. Her recorded year-long webinar series, Educators Living in the Joy of Gratitude, features global veteran educators' outcomes of sharing the principles for as much as 40 years in classrooms, school systems and student services. She has a MA from the University of Southern California and is adjunct faculty at the University of Minnesota.

Overview of My Guide Inside Comprehensive Curriculum

My Guide Inside, Book III offers Stories and Activities Designed for Success
Reading Level: "Advanced Fluent" (age 13-19)
Flexibility: regular course or adapt or modify to suit individual learners
Settings: classroom, small group or individual
Design: inclusive of self-directed learners working independently
Digital Media: Resources at myguideinside.com Video On Demand for each chapter
Ideal Time: start of a program or school year to build community and foster optimism

Objectives of *My Guide Inside (Book III)*: The principles discussed in this learner book operate in all people, including every teen. This *MGI* curriculum points the way to wholeness, happiness, creativity and well-being in all parts of life.
Therefore, *MGI* has these two globally appropriate academic goals:
(1) to enhance Personal Well-being with an understanding of these principles, and **(2) to develop competencies in Communication, Thinking, and Personal and Social Awareness and Responsibility.**
MGI accomplishes both goals by using stories, discussion and various written and creative activities, as it increases competency in English Language Arts, including Digital Media.

Discovering their guide inside is key to learning, and it enhances children's ability to make decisions, navigate life, and build healthy relationships. Accessing this natural wisdom affects well-being, spiritual wellness, personal and social responsibility, and positive personal and cultural identity. Social and emotional learning, including self-determination, self-regulation, and self-efficacy, is also a natural outcome of greater awareness of one's own inner wisdom/"guide inside." This understanding maximizes personal well-being and improves school climate, learner behavior, and academic performance. See Focus Group Experiences with My Guide Inside video of secondary student outcomes: 5min overview or full 27min interview myguideinside.com.

Learning, Living, Sharing: The feeling a *MGI* teacher brings to the classroom every day, the "essential curriculum," is the greatest resource for directly impacting students. In other words, learning allows a teacher to live the principles by being in a natural state of service; sharing compassion, understanding and joy in the classroom. Once a teacher is being that informally and naturally, the teacher will be sharing the principles, via a positive feeling. This will enhance and make more powerful any formal lesson sharing with students. A teacher's own deep understanding and experience of these principles will bring out the best in all students. As each teacher continually learns and lives the principles, sharing this understanding with students becomes highly effective.

The Teacher's Manual for each book contains lesson plans, pre- and post-assessments, activities, evaluation scales, and online resources. Based on universal principles, this curriculum is designed for global use with all learners. Curriculum guidelines from Canada, the United Kingdom, and the United States guide this work.

Instructional Materials for Pre K – 12 Learners

My Guide Inside **Pre-K -12 Comprehensive Curriculum**
Campsall, C. with Marshall Emerson, K. (2018). *My Guide Inside, Learner Book I.*
Campsall, C. with Marshall Emerson, K. (2018). *My Guide Inside, Teacher's Manual, Book I.*
Campsall, C., Tucker, J. (2016). *My Guide Inside, Learner Book II.*
Campsall, C. with Marshall Emerson, K. (2017). *My Guide Inside, Teacher's Manual, Book II.*
Campsall, C. (2017). with Marshall Emerson, K. *My Guide Inside, Learner Book III.*
Campsall, C. with Marshall Emerson, K. (2017). *My Guide Inside, Teacher's Manual, Book III.*
Picture Book (Pre-K)
Campsall, C., Tucker, J. (2018). *Whooo ... has a Guide Inside?*
Supplemental Books for Parents and Educators
Marshall Emerson, K. (2020). *Parenting With Heart.*
Tucker, J. (2020). *Insights: Messages of Hope, Peace and Love.*

My Guide Inside is available through myguideinside.com
Check the website for:
E-books, MGI Online for schools, Video On Demand, Resources, Translations and More...

My Guide Inside® Comprehensive Curriculum

well-being *communication*
responsibility *resilience* *relationships*
academic success
happiness
self-efficacy

My Guide Inside (MGI) is designed to bring out the best in all students. A senior completing *My Guide Inside* classes wisely said…

"Mental wellness needs to be part of every school district's policies because if students are in a place where they do not feel they are capable to learn and don't have that emotional capacity to learn, school is not going to be successful."

For other My Guide Inside offerings, see
myguideinside.com

www.ingramcontent.com/pod-product-compliance
Lightning Source LLC
Chambersburg PA
CBHW042024150426
43198CB00002B/58